KEELA
a slater brothers novella

AMAZON BESTSELLING AUTHOR

L. A. CASEY

Keela
a slater brothers novella
Copyright © 2015 by L.A. Casey
Published by L.A. Casey
www.lacaseyauthor.com

Cover Design by Mayhem Cover Creations | Editing by Gypsy Heart Editing
Formatting by JT Formatting

This book is licensed for your personal enjoyment only. This book may not be re-sold or given away to other people. If you would like to share this book with another person, please purchase an additional copy for each recipient. If you're reading this book and did not purchase it, or it wasn't purchased for your use only, then please return to your favorite book retailer and purchase your own copy. Thank you for respecting the hard work of this author.

All rights reserved.

Except as permitted under S.I. No. 337/2011 – European Communities (Electronic Communications Networks and Services) (Universal Service and Users' Rights) Regulations 2011, no part of this publication may be reproduced, distributed, or transmitted in any form or by any means, or stored in a database or retrieval system, without prior written permission of the author. The scanning, uploading, and distribution of this book via the Internet or via other means without the permission of the publisher is illegal and punishable by law. Please purchase only authorized electronic editions and do not participate in or encourage electronic piracy of copyrighted materials. This is a work of fiction. Names, characters, places, brands, media, and incidents are either the product of the author's imagination or are used fictitiously. The author acknowledges the trademarked status and trademark owners of various products referenced in this work of fiction, which have been used without permission. The publication/use of these trademarks is not authorized, associated with, or sponsored by the trademark owners.

Keela / L.A. Casey – 1st ed.
ISBN-13: 978-1507553190 | ISBN-10: 1507553196

DEDICATION

Nanny,

I miss you. I miss you terribly. It's been fourteen days since you left us, and I still can't accept that you aren't here anymore. I'm still expecting my ma to ring and tell me to get ready because we're going up to the hospital to see you. In a way I like thinking that, I like thinking you're up in the hospital because that would mean you're still here, even though deep down I know you're gone on to a better place. While I'm sad you're no longer here, I'm so happy you're out of pain and at peace. I'm *so* unbelievably happy you're at peace. God knows I am. You're up in the land above with Granda, Jason, Auntie Kay, and Tanya. God must not know what to do with himself with you lot up there together. I can only imagine the mischief you all get up to! LOL.

I watch the videos I took of you in the hospital every day just to see you and hear your voice. I cry laughing at them, you had us all in tears of laughter that night from the things you were saying. I'm so glad I recorded it, I would forget half the things you said otherwise. It makes me feel better to watch those videos, to remember the good times. To be honest, I thought I would be fine once you passed on. I was so sure I would be happy you're finally resting, and I am, but I'm not at the same time. I just miss you. I can't even talk to anyone about it because I don't want to upset them because they love and miss you just as much as I do. It's all a process, I know that. It will take getting used to, you being gone. It just sucks.

I know you're with me though. You're my number one supporter when it comes to my writing. You told everyone about my books, and you didn't care if they were interested or not, you still told them all about my career so far and about all the signings and places I've been to, and places I'm going. You're proud of me, you told me so and it was honestly the best thing you could have ever said to me. I'm now living by what you told me, you told me to *go for it*, and I am. I promise you I'll go for every opportunity presented to me and grab it with both hands.

It is an absolute pleasure to call you my nanny. I don't think grandmothers come better than you. You're one of a kind, and I just want you to know that you're deeply loved and I will never forget you. Not ever. You know I dedicated *Frozen* to you, you loved that, but it feels right to dedicate *Keela* to you too, even though you would lose your mind if you got to read what was on the pages of a *Slater Brothers* book. LOL.

I'll love you forever.

This isn't goodbye, it's I'll see you later <3

TABLE OF CONTENTS

Chapter One	1
Chapter Two	18
Chapter Three	29
Chapter Four	39
Chapter Five	46
Chapter Six	52
Chapter Seven	65
Chapter Eight	78
Chapter Nine	84
Chapter Ten	91
Chapter Eleven	104
Chapter Twelve	112
Chapter Thirteen	120

Chapter Fourteen	127
KANE – Chapter One	132
Acknowledgements	138
About the Author	140
Other Titles	141

CHAPTER ONE

"Keela... Help me."

I opened my eyes and sat upright from my laid down position. I wasn't in my bedroom, or even in my apartment. I was somewhere I had been before, but I couldn't identify where. It was a collection of hallways with a number of closed doors.

Fear gripped me, and I began to breathe hard as I stood up. "Keela?"

The voice was in my ear urging me for help, begging me with each faint breath. It caused my heart to speed up. I spun around in a circle to see who needed me, but found no source of the voice.

"Where are you?" I shouted.

I heard a male cry out, and it fightened me. I *knew* that cry, but I couldn't think of who it belonged to. My mind was a cloud of confusion.

I started to run through the darkened hallways. I turned left then right then left again as I zoomed down the hallways in search of the person calling out for me. Each hallway wall was identical to the next, and I wasn't sure if I took a wrong turn and was somehow back to where I was when I opened my eyes. Everything was horrifyingly similar to me. I knew I walked these hallways before, but I couldn't remember when or why.

I screeched when the cream coloured hallway walls surrounding me began to change colour. I tilted my head to the side and watched as blood trails appeared on the walls in the form of human handprints. It looked like someone had placed their bloody hand on the wall and leisurely walked down the hallway smearing the deep red liquid along the way.

I screamed with fright and began to run again.

"Keela?" the voice from before shouted out.

It came from every direction like there was surround sound in the hallway.

"Who are you?" I screamed in dismay. "*Where* are you?"

Suddenly everything went deathly silent.

The only sound I could pick up on was that of my own hasty breathing.

I stopped moving and listened.

After a few moments of absolute silence, I heard a lock click. The sound sent vibrations through the floor under my feet, and for a moment I thought I would fall over with the force of it. The vibrations stopped as quickly as they started, and I managed to regain my balance. The creak and whine of a door being opened filled my ears seconds later and I whirled around to see who or what was behind it. I squinted my eyes when a door down the end of hallway opened wide, but all I could see inside was darkness.

"Wh-who's there?" I called out, my voice aquiver.

I heard a male whine, then a metallic click sound—it was one that I *was* familiar with. It was the sound of the hammer of a gun being pulled back.

I swallowed down the bile that threatened to spew up my throat at that moment.

"Keela?" a familiar female voice whispered from behind me. "You have to help Alec."

Alec?

I spun around, but like before, there was no one there.

"Alec?" I called out.

"Keela!" his voice screamed.

I felt myself fall into a panic when I recognised it was Alec's voice I'd heard earlier. His voice was the voice filled with pain and fear that was calling out to me for help minutes before.

"Where are you?" I screamed.

"In there, you have to help him," the female voice whispered in my ear as I turned to the door that lead into darkness. Without a single thought I began to run towards the dark room, but no matter how fast I ran, the room never got any closer to me.

I screamed and jumped back with fright when a shadowy figure appeared in front of me. I fell onto my behind and screeched in terror when the figure shot forward and got in my face.

I could only see glowing silver eyes, no face or features.

"Alec will die unless you stop her," the figure before me whispered.

"Stop *who*?" I screamed.

The figure faded away to nothing and I once again had a view of the darkened room, only it wasn't dark anymore. It was lit up, and Alec was in the middle of the room on his knees reaching out for me, but his head was bowed. I blinked and when I focused my eyes the shadow figure re-appeared, but was now standing behind Alec.

"Stop her, Keela!" the female voice screamed at me from every direction. "Fight to save him!"

I gasped when the figure lifted its arm and pointed the object in its hand at Alec's bowed head. I squinted my eyes to see what it was and when the silver barrel of a gun caught my eye I jumped to my feet. I screamed for Alec to watch out as I ran towards him. This time when I ran towards the room it got closer, but even at my fastest sprint I still wasn't quick enough.

"Alec!" I screamed when a loud noise ripped through the hallway and rang in my ears.

The gun went off and Alec's body fell limp to the floor at the same time the door of the room slammed shut. I reached the door a second later and crashed into it. I felt no physical pain as I bounced off the door and fell back onto the floor. I could feel nothing over the gripping pain in my chest, and the tears streaming down my face.

I got back to my feet and tried to open the door, but the doorknob wouldn't turn. I slapped on the door with both of my hands and kicked it with my feet, but to no avail. It was locked tight.

"Keela?" another familiar voice spoke to me from behind.

I turned around and gasped.

Nico, Ryder, Damien, and Kane were stood before me.

"You have to help—"

"Why didn't you save our brother, Keela?" Damien cut me off.

I blinked. "I tried—"

"You let Alec die. You let our brother die," Nico cut me off as he glared at me.

I began to pant as I took a small step backwards, however I bumped into the door I'd ruthlessly tried to open only seconds before.

"I ran. I tried to—"

"You let him die because you don't want him, you don't want his life," Ryder cut me off.

His voice was a growl.

"No!" I began to whimper. "I love Alec, I want him. Please, help me help him."

Kane clicked his tongue at me. "He loved you, Keela. He wanted to marry you, and you let him die. Why?"

I closed my eyes.

"Why didn't you want our brother?"

"Why didn't you save him?"

"Why didn't you love him?"

"Why, Keela?"

I placed my hands over my ears and screamed to block out the voices of the Slater brothers, but I heard each of them clearly in my head.

Why? Why? Why? Why?

I opened my eyes and screamed even louder when the four brothers rushed at me with extended arms. I dropped to my knees and bowed my head and waited for the pain of their attack to come, but it never did. I hesitantly looked up and cried out when the hallways dropped away along with the brothers. Everything had been replaced by a large room with a huge circular platform in the centre. Two faceless males were fighting up on it, and crowds of people surrounded the platform screaming and cheering them on.

I got to my feet as I looked around the room and took everything in. The platform, the people, the dance floor, the booths, the bar... I knew where I was... I was in Darkness.

"Keela? Come here, darlin'."

I spun around and stared at my uncle Brandon.

"Why?... How?..."

"Shhh," my uncle Brandon murmured as he walked over to me. "It's all goin' to be okay. I'll make everythin' better."

I turned to him and hugged him, but pulled back when his hands pressed against my back and the feeling of wetness struck me. I stepped away from my grinning uncle and placed my hands on my back. I brought my hands back around to my front and stared down at them.

They were stained with a thick red liquid.

I whimpered when the metallic twang of blood filled my nose. I looked back up to my uncle, but screamed and stumbled backwards when the person in front of me was not my uncle. It was the ghost of a devil from my past.

"Marco," I whimpered.

Marco Miles evilly smiled at me, and looked down to his hands. His *blood* covered hands.

He clicked his tongue and lifted his gaze to meet mine.

"Well... isn't this interesting?"

I tried to back away from him, but multiple hands clamped down on my body and forced me down to my knees. I looked up, then to my left and right and wailed.

Nico and Damien held me down on my right, and Ryder and Kane held me down on my left.

"Now," Nico growled. "Make her pay for hurting Alec."

"I didn't hurt him! It wasn't me!" I screamed. "It was the shadow!"

The familiar click of a gun being cocked infiltrated my mind.

I felt the shock of a cold metal object being pressed against my forehead. I was hyperventilating with sobs as I lifted my head and stared down the barrel of a handgun. I screamed in terror when the culprit holding the gun wasn't Marco, but the shadow figure.

"You!" I bellowed as tears flowed down my cheeks. "Why are you doin' this?"

The shadow figure solidified and became a person. The person was dressed in a long black cloak with a large hood covering their face.

"Answer me," I screamed and struggled against the brothers' hold on me.

The shadow person lifted their free hand and tugged back the hood.

I froze as I stared at my own reflection.

It was me.

I was the shadow figure.

"You don't deserve him," the shadow version of me said and pulled the trigger.

I awoke with a jolt, panting and covered in sweat. I needed to sit up so I could breathe, but I couldn't.

I was being crushed.

Crushed to death by a muscular sixteen stone male.

It wasn't Storm either.

My fiancé, the bear who was crushing the life out of me, easily had seventy percent of his large body spread out over me, pinning me to my mattress. I was used to this—Alec rarely let go of me when we slept, but at times when I had to wee so bad I could have cried, it was horrible.

Right now was one of those times.

I didn't want to wake Alec because he needed his full eight hours of sleep, otherwise he reverted back to a grumpy toddler. I also didn't want him to see me in my current state.

I was always a wreck after having the nightmare.

I tried to press myself back into my mattress to create a dent for some space so it would make slipping out of the bed easier. When I moved though, Alec's arm only tightened around my body.

Oh, for fuck's sake.

I had to get up.

"Alec," I grunted.

Nothing.

"Alec."

Not a bloody peep.

"ALEC!"

Alec jolted awake, jumped upright and brought my duvet with him in his panic. Now that I was free from his crushing weight I quickly rolled to my left and stood up off my bed and onto the floor. I rolled my neck on my shoulders and stretched my arms and legs out.

That felt better, *much* better.

"Are you okay? What's wrong?" Alec asked as he crawled over the bed to me in a blind panic.

He kneeled on our mattress and placed his hands on my shoulders. It was dark in our room, but the light from the hallway shone in and helped me see Alec's handsome face. I watched as his eyes squinted and scanned over my face through the darkness. He pushed me out to arms length and looked down my body, his eyes scrutinising every inch of me. He let me go after a moment and sat back on his heels with a frown on his tired face.

"You look okay," he muttered.

I couldn't help but smile. "I *am* okay."

That was the furthest thing from the truth.

Alec stared at me for a long moment before he growled, "Why did you shout my name then?"

Because you were crushing me to death.

I shrugged. "I needed to use the toilet and you were pinnin' me to the bed so I called your name to wake you up," I lied.

Alec deadpanned, "You didn't just 'Call my name', you shouted it like you were being murdered."

An image of the gun going off in my nightmare struck me, but I shook it off.

"I would have screeched or at the very least given a high-pitched white-woman scream if I was being murdered. I wouldn't have shouted at all if I knew it would have upset you this much."

Alec looked exhausted as he rubbed his hand over his gorgeous face. "Why a white-woman?"

I shrugged, again. "It's usually the white ones who scream the loudest that get killed in the slasher films."

Alec blinked his tired eyes then turned away from me and fell back down onto his side of the bed.

Nice talk.

I turned and scurried out of the bedroom, down the hallway, and into the bathroom. I relieved myself and sighed in delight while doing so. After I finished my business I moved to the sink and washed my hands. I splashed some water on my face and stared into the mirror.

"It was only a dream," I told myself.

When I emerged from the bathroom, I turned my head in the direction of the kitchen and sitting room and listened. I relaxed and went back to my bedroom when I heard Storm's reassuring snores.

I was like a mama bear when it came to him, even more so after he was hurt last year. Every time I used the toilet at night I always listened out to make sure I heard his snores so I knew he was still breathing. It relaxed me knowing he was okay.

Once back inside my bedroom I crawled into my bed and snuggled into my pillow. I covered myself with my duvet and closed my eyes on a relaxed sigh. I opened them not a second later when I felt something graze against my behind.

I instantly narrowed my eyes. "Don't even think about it."

Silence.

I didn't move my body, but I did open my eyes and concentrated as I listened for Alec's movements. I heard nothing but his breathing and frowned.

Maybe it *was* the duvet that touched—"Alec!" I shouted, interrupting my thoughts.

Alec chuckled like a youngster as he wrapped his arms around my body and pulled me backwards until my back was moulded into his front. He rolled his pelvis into my behind and as soon as I felt the hardness of his length I knew sleeping was out of the question. I allowed him to turn me onto my back, and I could sense his smile when I turned my head and kissed the closest part of his body my mouth could reach, which turned out to be his collarbone.

"I knew it was you who touched me," I murmured.

Alec leaned down and brushed his nose against mine. "Whenever something touches a part of your body when we're in bed, it's a ninety-nine-point-nine percent chance it's me, not Storm, looking to cop a feel."

I lightly snickered. "I can never be sure, a few times Storm has come into the room and nudged me as he snuck up onto the bed."

Alec scoffed. "An overweight German Shepherd shouldn't be able to sneak anywhere. I'm serious about setting up cameras to see how he's so stealthy when he's creeping around."

Joy filled me as Alec's antics pushed away the worry and nagging fear leftover from my nightmare.

I grinned. "He is a ninja dog."

My new codename for Storm grated on Alec's nerves.

"Ninja dog, please. More like suspicious dog. I swear he was a human in his past life."

I laughed then and flung my hand over my mouth to keep quiet.

"Why are you being quiet?" Alec asked. "It's only us here."

I nodded in the direction of the hallway. "Storm's asleep."

Alec hated when I was quiet in our bedroom.

He groaned. "A man shouldn't have to worry about keeping his woman quiet in the bedroom, he should worry if she's not loud enough."

I smiled, but remained quiet.

"Are you going to spread your legs and give yourself to me... or are you going to make me beg?"

I pretended to think on it.

"Come on, Kitten, I only have God knows how long before we have kids and sex is nothing but a fond memory in the back of my mind."

I bit down on my lower lip as I reached out and placed my hand on Alec's bicep. I ran it all the way up to his shoulder then curved it around the back of his neck and pulled his head down to mine.

I gave him a whisper soft kiss then murmured, "Do you think you can make me scream, Playboy?"

"I fucking know I can," Alec growled.

Then, like a snap of my fingers, he was between my legs.

I licked my lips and lifted my pelvis up so Alec could slide my underwear from my body.

"I don't understand why you even bother to wear these to bed," Alec muttered to himself as he flung my knickers over his shoulder.

I rid myself of my tank top and tossed it somewhere in the room. I was naked, and spread wide as I waited for Alec. He reached over and flipped on the lamp on his bedside locker so he could see me. He squinted for a moment then smiled down at me with his big blue eyes when he could see me clearly.

"There's my pretty Kitten."

I flushed.

Alec then scooted back a little and lowered his head to my pooch aka my stomach.

I groaned when he kissed the spot above my belly button. "Why is it always me belly you kiss first? The one part of me body I hate and you—"

"Show you that I love it just the way it is."

Silence.

Damn him for being so bloody cute.

"It's fat. *I'm* fat."

Alec looked up at me with pained eyes then moved up my body until he was resting on his elbows as he hovered over me. "Are we going to have this talk *again*?"

Yes.

I shrugged. "I've gained a stone since we started datin', don't try and tell me I haven't gotten bigger. I *know* I have, me favourite pair of jeans not buttonin' up anymore is a clear sign."

Alec leaned his face down and brushed his nose over mine. "You aren't fat, you gained some weight, but not enough to even border on being fat. You look healthy."

I scoffed and gripped my belly pooch.

"Explain this?"

Alec looked down and rolled his eyes. "That is just some excess skin from when you were heavier a few years ago. Not everyone's skin snaps back when they lose weight, you know?"

Tell me about it.

I grunted, "Yeah, I know."

I had the pooch to prove how well I knew.

Alec kissed my forehead. "You're beautiful, inside and outside, with or without your excess—"

"Pooch," I corrected.

Alec snorted. "With or without your *pooch*."

I furrowed my eyebrows. "You say that now until a perfectly toned woman or man walks by and you wonder why you aren't with him or her instead of stumpy me."

Alec cursed. "Stop it, you're going to piss me off with that stupid way of thinking. I love *you*. I'm engaged to *you*. I'm going to have children some day with *you*. No one else. You're it for me and that is the last time I ever want to hear you doubting that, do you understand me Keela?"

I blinked up at Alec.

"Say you understand," he said, his tone firm.

I licked my lips. "I understand."

Alec leaned down and brushed his lips against mine. "What's that heated look you're giving me?"

Lust, love, and admiration.

"I'm so hot for you."

Alec raised his eyebrows. "Oh, really?"

I nodded my head.

Alec grinned and pecked my lips before he moved down my body and kissed every patch of skin he could along the way including my pooch. He palmed my breasts and pressed his nose against my mound and inhaled.

I hated when he did that.

"It's a vagina not a bloody flower, enough with the damn sniffin' already!" I hissed.

I heard him chuckle and felt the vibrations against my flesh. I bit down on my lower lip when he spread me with his tongue and circled my clit.

Fuck.

My hips began to involuntarily rise upwards, but Alec clamped his hands down on my hips, and not so gently pulled me back down until I was once again lying flat on our bed. I licked my lips and fisted the bed sheets in my hands as Alec suckled and licked me until my breathing was fast and audible.

"Oh, God," I groaned as he shook his head from left to right.

I hissed as Alec brushed his stubble against me and clicked my tongue in disapproval when he lightly chuckled at me. He continued to torture me as he slid his hands from my hips upwards back towards my breasts. He palmed them and tweaked my nipples as he sucked my clit back into his mouth and rubbed his lips back and forth over it causing my back to arch.

"There! There! There!" I repeated in breathless pants as sizzling pulses were pulled from every corner of my body and sucked, literally, to the hot spot between my legs.

When my orgasm hit I opened my mouth and silent cries flew free. My eyes rolled back, my toes curled, and shivers shot up and down my spine. For an unknown amount of seconds I was unaware of my surroundings, time, and life itself. I was lost in bliss... and the bliss only continued when I came to, just as my man lined his cock up against my entrance and thrust forward.

"Every time," Alec hissed as he shivered in pleasure. "You feel like ecstasy *every single time*."

I wrapped my legs around his hips and raised my arms above my head so he could grab my wrists and pin them there. He didn't realise it, but he liked having that bit of control over me during sex so I offered it up to him freely. I lifted my head to his when he lowered the upper half of his body down to me.

"Make me sore," I whispered.

Alec growled as he bit down on my cheek before he slid his teeth over my flesh and nipped at my lips, which hurt in a delicious way. He pulled out of me and thrust right back in as he fell into a slow and steady rhythm of fucking me. I arched my back so his chest brushed against my nipples with his every thrust.

"Talk to me," Alec growled.

I flicked my eyes up to his and found they were ablaze for me. *Only me.*

"I can feel you... so *deep* inside me," I whispered, and purposely stuck my tongue out and slid it over my lips in a slow seductive invitation for him to kiss me.

Alec growled as he slammed into me making me gasp. He covered my mouth with his at that exact moment and took my gasp as his own and swallowed it down. He let go of one of my wrists and lowered his now free hand to my head, where he fisted my thick red mane in his hand and pulled.

I hissed, not in pain but in approval.

"I want your ass," he said with his eyes locked on mine.

He was looking for any hesitation or worry in my eyes. I knew if he saw the slightest hint of either one, he wouldn't take my arse like he wanted, he would just continue to fuck me the way he already was. I wasn't worried about anal sex, but I *was* worried for our future sex life if I didn't enjoy it. We had tried it once before, and it didn't last long enough for me to judge if I liked it or not, so a round of arse fucking was something I was heartedly game for, and something I had been waiting for.

"Take it then," I challenged Alec who smirked at me as he plunged into me for a long, deep stroke.

I moaned in delight then whimpered when he pulled out of me.

"Bold man," I hissed.

Alec grinned as he slapped my thigh and said, "Roll over."

I did as ordered and rolled onto my front. I pressed my hands into the mattress and pushed up my upper body while my bent knees held up my lower half. I swayed my hips from left to right in invitation.

I looked over my shoulder to Alec whose gaze was locked on my arse.

I smirked. "What are you waitin' for?" I asked.

Alec flicked his eyes to mine and glared.

He slapped my arse, hard.

I yelped.

"Don't rush me with this, I don't want to hurt you."

"You just slapped me," I argued.

He slapped my arse again.

"Only because you love it."

I kept my mouth shut and grinned—he knew me too well.

I felt the mattress move as Alec climbed off the bed and moved over to his side of the bed where he opened the top drawer of his bedside locker.

I closed my eyes and leaned my head down until it rested against the mattress. The pulsing between my thighs was starting to slow so I reached down between my legs and slid my fingers up and down my wet folds for a few strokes before I rotated them around my sensitive clit. I licked my lips as my hips bucked each my time my fingers made direct contact. I continued to tease myself until Alec moved away from his locker and moved to where I assumed was the end of the bed. I confirmed my assumption when I looked between my legs and saw him stood just a few feet away from me.

"Fuck me," he growled after a moment or two.

I inwardly glowed and closed my eyes.

He was watching me.

I could *feel* his eyes on me.

"Damn, Kitten," he breathed and climbed up onto the bed behind me.

I felt his hands clamp down on my hips, then his pelvis brush against me.

"If it's too painful, tell me. Okay?" Alec ordered, his tone stern.

I nodded my head and pushed my behind into him.

He hissed.

I flinched a little when a cold gel was spread out over my anus then couldn't help but tense as Alec gently slid his finger inside me. I felt him stop so I forced myself to relax. I exhaled a large breath and let the tension seep out of my muscles until I was loose and relaxed.

Alec gently stretched me out with his finger for a bit, then added a second, then a third and to be honest, it didn't feel good. It just felt like someone was sticking their fingers up my arse, which is exactly what he was doing. I refused to give up so soon though, instead I focused on my breathing and tried not to think about it.

"Do you want to play with your clit?" Alec asked me.

Yes!

"Can I?" I asked.

Alec chuckled and used his free hand to slap my arse.

"Yes, bring yourself to the edge for me, but don't make yourself come until I tell you to."

I did as told and played with my clit enough to make me pant, but not come. I stroked my finger over my clit and shivered. Alec chose this moment to press the head of his cock into my arse. I groaned as he pushed past the thick ring of muscle and fully embedded himself inside me.

"Okay?" he asked.

It hurt, but not that bad.

Alec on the other hand sounded like he was hurting terribly.

"I'm fine," I breathed. "Are you okay?"

He slowly pulled out halfway, then eased back into me. "It's too... fucking... good."

I purred with delight and gently pushed back as Alec thrust forward into me.

"Oh my God," he breathed.

I couldn't help but laugh. "You sound like you're goin' to cry."

"I could," he hissed. "It feels... perfect. *You* feel perfect."

I hummed with pleasure.

I continued to play with my clit, and after a minute or two Alec couldn't keep to his slow and steady thrusts and began to pump into my body harder and faster. I was surprised with the pleasure it brought me.

"Yes," I groaned.

Alec slid his hands to my arse cheeks and squeezed them. "I wish you could see this."

I imagined watching his cock sliding in and out of me, and the erotic image only fuelled my pleasure as I worked my fingers faster against my pulsing clit.

"Keela," Alec gasped.

I knew that gasp... he was close.

"Now!" He shouted. "Make yourself come!"

I pushed back harder against him and worked my fingers faster. Six pumps later and my mind went blank as waves of pleasure spread from my clit, to my arse and back again.

"Yes!" I screamed and rode out the sensations.

I think Alec called out my name as his fast movements slowed to short jerky thrusts of his pelvis.

My upper body was flat against my mattress, and once Alec stopped grinding into me, my lower body joined my upper half flat on the bed a second before Alec collapsed on top of me. He semi slid off my body leaving his legs hanging off the end of the bed, while his upper body was sprawled out across my back.

"Was... that... good... for you?" Alec asked, breathing rapidly against my spine.

I was trapped under him and couldn't move even if I wanted to.

I was spent.

I grunted in response.

"What does... that mean?" Alec asked, still regaining his breath as he nuzzled his face against my skin.

He was exhausted, yet I could hear the worry in his voice.

I smiled into my mattress. "It means when you get your breath back, can we do that again?"

Alec was silent for a moment then he laughed, hard.

He kissed my lower back. "God, I love you."

"I love you, too," I murmured. "I'm serious though, I wanna do that again."

Alec vibrated with laughter. "Give me a minute."

"Fifty-nine, fifty-eight, fifty-seven—"

Alec's glorious laughter cut me off causing my insides to beam with happiness. I closed my eyes then and prayed that I would wake up feeling as happy. I prayed my dreaded nightmare would be kept at bay.

CHAPTER TWO

I was asleep until I felt a poke on my behind rousing me from my peaceful slumber.

"Kitten?" a voice whispered.

I didn't know if I was dreaming or not so I remained still and murmured, "Hmmm?"

I felt a harder nudge on my backside and my body tensed up.

Definitely not dreaming.

Oh, no, not right now.

"Go into the bathroom and get yourself off," I said then stretched my body out, lightly tensing when soreness gripped my behind.

Alec halted touching me as he said, "What?"

I groaned, "We *just* had sex—me vagina, and arse, are closed until further notice. Feck off."

Alec chuckled, "We had sex seven hours ago, but that's not why I'm waking you up."

Seven hours ago?

It felt like I was asleep for less than a minute.

"What are you wakin' me up for if not for sex?" I asked, pestered.

A suspicion niggled at the back of my mind that he was up to something.

I felt Alec get out of bed, but I didn't move or open my eyes.

He cleared his throat. "It's moving day, I'm going to go and get the moving truck in an hour with Kane."

Brilliant.

"You go and do that."

Silence.

"Keela?"

I pressed myself down into my mattress and whimpered.

"I thought you were leavin'?"

Alec exhaled loudly. "You *have* to get up and start boxing up the things you want to keep and things you want to trash... I *told* you we should have started packing over the weekend instead of leaving it until today."

Sorry, Mother.

I inwardly rolled my eyes.

"We live in a shoebox, how many things can we possibly have?" I asked without moving or opening my eyes.

I mentally winced once the question passed my lips.

Alec snorted. "You're the Queen of hoarding so trust me, we have *a lot* of crap."

I didn't like to throw things out that could be of future use, so sue me!

I knew I had to get up and get a move on, but I didn't move from the bed and it must have annoyed Alec.

"Get up or I'm pulling a Branna and pouring water all over you," he threatened.

I didn't bother laughing or saying something enticing because he would do it—the evil bastard.

"I'm up, I'm up... you miserable sod," I grumbled.

I opened my eyes and looked up to Alec when he walked around to my side of the bed. I smiled as he gazed down at me. I stood up and ran my hands up his bare arms until they slid up his shoulders and neck and were buried in his hair.

He was stunning.

He was *mine*.

"I can't believe you're goin' to cut your hair," I said, frowning.

Alec leaned forward and kissed my forehead. "I know."

I tugged on it. "Don't do it."

Alec sighed, "I lost a bet, Keela. The terms were if I lost the bet then I had to get a buzz cut."

I shivered. "Don't get a buzz cut... can you not just get a tiny trim?"

Alec smiled and shook his head.

I growled, "I hate your brother for makin' you do this."

Alec laughed and leaned his face down to mine. "I'm not Dominic's biggest fan right now either, Kitten, but a deal is a deal."

I grumbled, "Stupid fuckin' bets."

I loathed bets, and for good reason too.

The last time I was involved in a bet my life exploded into a very bad Irish version of *The Godfather*.

Alec chuckled again, pecked my lips and hugged me to him. "I'll get a short buzz cut on the sides of my head then leave the hair long enough on top that you can still knot your fingers in it. It will meet the terms of the bet since Dominic never said I had to get a full buzz cut, he said just a buzz cut. I'll pick up the truck then get it done, okay?"

Nice.

I snickered, "It's not *me* you should be tryin' to accommodate. You *know* Aideen loves your hair, she does be delighted when you let her style and plait it. You're her very own human Ken doll."

Alec smiled. "I let her do that just because she likes it and it keeps her quiet... besides, it will be long enough that she can still play around with it. I'll explain it to her."

An explanation? Ha.

That wouldn't be good enough for Aideen Collins.

I harshly chewed on my inner cheek. "She may kill Nico for this."

Alec grinned. "I'm fine with him getting roughed up a bit."

"I didn't say he would get roughed up a bit, I said she may *kill* him."

Alec snickered. "I'll talk about it with her."

I nodded my head. "Good, because I'm sure as hell not settin' foot in *that* death trap."

Alec raised his eyebrows. "You'd let me step foot in it though?"

Hell to the yes.

"Mate, when Aideen and her temper is involved in a situation, I'll throw you head first into any trap she sets. You best believe that."

Alec stared at me with wide, shocked eyes then tackled me back on our bed. I screamed with laughter and playfully struggled when he pinned me beneath him. He leaned his face down to mine and I giggled when the ends of his hair tickled my face.

"I'm going to miss your hair," I said for the umpteenth time since he told me last week that he had to cut his hair.

Alec lovingly kissed my nose. "It'll grow back."

"I know, but still," I murmured and lifted my hands to his head and ran my fingers through his hair.

Alec chuckled when I stuck my bottom lip out and pouted.

"It's only hair, baby."

To him, maybe.

I shrugged my shoulders. "I've never seen you with short hair... I may find you ugly."

Alec applied a large amount of his weight down on me when he started to laugh.

"Crushin' me," I rasped and slapped Alec's back because my chest started to burn from lack of oxygen.

Alec continued to laugh as he leaned up off me. He brushed his nose against mine again then pecked my lips before he stood up off me completely.

"C'mon, up you get," he chirped.

This again?

I groaned. "You suck!"

Alec looked down at me when I stood up from the bed in front of him.

"You do the sucking in this relationship, sweetheart." He grinned, wickedly.

I narrowed my teasing eyes. "And you do the kissin'... *arse* kissin'."

Literally *and* figuratively.

Alec winked. "Only when I'm naughty."

I grunted then smiled when he tickled the side of my mouth with his finger.

I hated when he did that.

I snapped my teeth at him making him retract his fingers to a safe distance away from my choppers. I grinned as I turned around and made a move to grab my duvet so I could shake it out and make my bed, only to find I couldn't because Storm was lying on top of it.

I didn't even hear him come in.

"Hello, my baby boy," I cooed.

Alec gasped from behind me. "How does he fucking *do* that?"

I smiled as I leaned over and scratched behind Storm's ears. "Because he is a cool dog."

"This is not funny, he doesn't make a fucking sound... it's not right, not right at all!"

I grinned. "I told you," I said as I turned around to face Alec again. "He is a ninja dog."

Alec huffed and leaned to the right and lifted his hand to his face, pointed two fingers at his eyes then pointed the same two fingers at Storm. "I'm watching you, big man."

Storm farted in response.

I burst out laughing then fled the room before the death like smell filled my nose.

"Damn dog," Alec muttered as he quickly followed me out of

the room, and down the hallway. "In the new house he isn't staying in-side, he will learn to sleep outside in the backyard in his dog house."

Yeah, like *that* would ever happen.

"Alec, there is a better chance of *you* sleeping in the dog house than Storm sleeping out there."

Alec muttered something to himself as he passed me and entered the kitchen.

"What was that?" I asked, smiling as I followed.

He glanced at me. "I said I wouldn't be surprised."

I cackled, "Good, because he is me baby. He was here *before* you were, big lad—don't forget that."

Alec looked at me and deadpanned, "How can I forget? When he is in the room and I even *attempt* to cop a feel he comes over and pushes his way between us. In dog speak, he tells me to back the fuck off his mama."

I burst out laughing.

"That's so true," I beamed.

Alec's lip quirked before he shook his head and looked down to the kitchen drawers. "Are you eating and then packing or packing then eating?"

Was that a serious question?

"Eatin' first... duh," I replied.

Alec blew out an extra amount of air from his nose as he smiled. "Sit down then, I'll make you something."

I shook my head. "Thanks for the offer, but I'm just goin' to have some yogurt and fruit."

Alec raised an eyebrow. "Why?"

I deadpanned, "I've been talkin' the past week about dietin'."

Did he listen to anything I say?

Alec glanced down at my body then back up to my head. "It's working, you look great."

He was so full of it.

"Oh, bite me!" I grunted. "I haven't lost any weight yet, you lick arse. Stop lookin' to get some extra points with your silly compliments."

Alec grinned. "I'm not fishin' for points, I was just *pointing out* that you look great. Even if you lose a little bit of weight you will *still* look great. What does that tell you?" he asked.

I shrugged my shoulders. "That you're a chubby chaser?"

Alec laughed. "No, smartass. It means you look great as is. Nothing you do can improve how beautiful you are, Kitten. You're naturally stunning."

I stared at Alec and snorted.

"I'm not having sex with you today."

"You say that everyday and guess what? We *still* have sex everyday... twice yesterday if I recall, three times if you include last night."

"I get it," I growled. "I have a weakness for your cock. No need to rub it in me face."

"There is always a need to rub my cock in your face."

Alec said this with a straight face and serious tone. I just laughed and shook my head. "Go get the movin' van and I'll get a start on packin'."

"It's a moving *truck*," Alec casually said as he walked by me and slapped my arse.

I yelped as a stinging pain spread across my behind. "It's a *van* here, not a truck. Get it right or I'm kickin' you out of the country."

Alec chuckled as he headed down the hallway to our bedroom where he got dressed. Not two minutes later he came back down the hallway fully clothed and he grabbed the keys to his recently bought SUV. The bloody thing was huge, but it was what he wanted so I didn't open my mouth. It was his money after all—he could buy whatever he wanted for himself.

I drew a line on what he could buy me though and that frustrated the hell out of him.

"I'll be back in an hour," he said and put on his coat.

I nodded my head as I opened the fridge door. "Drive safe."

"I always do," he said. "Love you."

I smiled as I scanned the contents of the fridge. "I love you, too."

With that said he was out the door and on his way to get Kane so they could get the moving van. I looked around my apartment and groaned out loud. I really wished I started packing during the week when Alec asked me to, but once I was in my writing cave, it was hard to drag me from it.

Alec knows that all too well.

I was going over edits for my first novel that I had been writing for the last year. I must have read the manuscript a million times, and each time I did re-writes. I changed something every single time I read it, whether it was a new sentence or a single word change and that freaked me out. I was worried in case I wouldn't be happy with the final product when I eventually self-published it so I kept putting it off.

I shook off the thoughts that have been worrying me lately and gazed out at my sitting room as I leaned against my kitchen counter. I swallowed down the sorrow that filled me. I have lived in this apartment since I was nineteen, and now I was going to be moving into a house so big my entire apartment could fit into the sitting room. Maybe not the *whole* sitting room, but definitely half of the downstairs.

Alec and I were moving to Upton... across the road from where his brothers and Branna lived. It was the exact same styled house, same layout, same number of bedrooms, same everything and it was facing the Slater/Murphy residence. It was too big for Alec, myself, and Storm, but Alec insisted when we had children the size would be perfect. It was a six-bedroom house, one was ours and that left five empty rooms. I don't know how many kids he planned on us having, but I wasn't a bloody oven. He couldn't just fill me up with his buns and set a cooking timer for nine months.

I groaned to myself and felt sick that I was having doubts. I didn't doubt Alec, I was just doubting how fast we were moving with our relationship. I knew him all of two weeks before we said I love you and got engaged. It wasn't even a whirlwind, love at first sight kind of romance either. I actually couldn't stand Alec when I met him, but I warmed up to him when he came to the Bahamas as a favour to me. His experience as an ex-escort served me well in the Bahamas, but it was also the cause for the heartbreak I felt after escaping the Bahamas.

Alec's past 'clients' caught up with him, and revealed some very... sickening information. It turned out a previous lover of Alec's was my uncle Brandon's wife, Everly, my cousin Micah's stepmother. That's not all, as if that knowledge wasn't migraine inducing enough, I found out my uncle had a shady side to him, a dirty and illegal side to him. I loved my uncle Brandon, God knows I did, but ever since learning his true colours back in the Bahamas, and watching men die in Darkness by his orders, I felt somewhat disconnected from him.

I felt like everything I thought I knew about him was a lie, that my life was a lie. Being in a brand new, fast paced relationship with Alec took up my time and thoughts, but now, thirteen months later, we were out of the 'honeymoon' stage of our relationship and I wasn't as wrapped up in him anymore.

I loved him dearly, but he wasn't acting as my shield to reality anymore. Everything that happened to me, to us, over a year ago was starting to stomp its way back into my mind, and it was starting to bother me. I would have nightmares of vile things I witnessed in Darkness, the dreaded club my uncle owned, a place I was taken to against my will by an old boss turned enemy of Alec and his brothers.

I would also have flashbacks of Alec and two people doing things that churned my stomach and hurt my heart with one single thought. I forgave Alec for that... situation. I understood that he had no other choice, and that he had to do something so gut wrenching so it would break us and force me away from him. My uncle ordered Alec to engage in sexual intercourse with his wife, and his new employee, Dante—an escort.

My uncle wanted me to have zero connections to any of the Slater brothers, especially Alec. By this time though, I was having strong feelings for Alec and wouldn't allow anyone to tell me that I couldn't have him. My defiance pushed my uncle's hand. He forced Alec to end things with me by threatening to harm his brothers and their girlfriends if Alec didn't do what he was told to do. Simply breaking up with me wasn't enough though—no, my uncle wanted me to hate Alec and he succeeded. For days after I left the Bahamas I hated Alec. I hated him for tricking me into falling for him. I hated him for breaking my heart. I hated him for a lot of reasons, but I mainly hated him for making me miss him.

God, I missed him so much that it hurt.

I was terrified about how intense my feelings were for someone who I barely knew, but I couldn't switch them off. Believe me, I tried. I didn't know it at the time, but I loved Alec, and I had to endure loving him and hating him at the same time. When Alec's old boss, Marco, came to seek revenge on Alec I was in the way so he kidnapped me along with Alec and Bronagh, Nico's girlfriend, who were in my apartment at the time. Long story short, Alec's brothers along with my uncle Brandon, saved us. Marco and his men died, and we were free to go home.

The problem is, now that I could see past Alec and his wonderful reality shield again, I didn't feel so free. I didn't feel trapped either, I just felt... restricted. I didn't know why I felt that way because Alec was my everything. I wanted to be with him... I just didn't want to rush things and inadvertently ruin things. We jumped headfirst into our relationship, and I felt like we needed to slow way down, but I was terrified to tell Alec any of this because I knew how it would sound.

It would sound like I wasn't certain about us anymore.

I sighed and shook my head clear of my thoughts, and like many times before, I forced them to the back of my mind and focused on the task at hand.

Packing.

A lot of packing.

"Damn it," I grumbled.

I placed my hands on my hips and shook my head.

This wasn't a one-woman job.

I walked into my sitting room and picked up my phone from the coffee table. I tapped on the screen of my phone, unlocked it, then scrolled through my contacts till I found the person I wanted to call.

I pressed my phone to my ear and after three rings the phone picked up. I glanced around my apartment once more and said, "It's me. I need your help."

CHAPTER THREE

"Hello? Royalty is in the house!"

I rolled my eyes and turned my head to my apartment door. "Close the door before Mr. Pervert comes out to see what all the racket is."

Aideen Collins, my best friend, rolled her hazel eyes and kicked my apartment door shut.

I hissed. "No damages. I won't get me deposit back from the landlord otherwise."

Aideen snorted as she dropped her bag and keys on my kitchen table and walked into my sitting room. "Please, money is the last thing you need to worry about. You're loaded."

I wasn't loaded with money—Alec was.

"I'm broke, Alec is not. Learn the difference."

Aideen grinned. "Alec would give you whatever you wanted, you know that. Money isn't an issue with him."

"I don't need or want his money, and it *will* be an issue if one of us doesn't earn a steady income. Sure, Alec has a lot of money in the bank, but it won't last forever. Not with the way he spends it anyway."

Aideen chuckled, "I don't think an SUV and a house will break his bank account."

I shook my head. "The house was three hundred and twenty thousand outright, and the only reason we got it at that price was because the buyers wanted a quick sale. Then there was his SUV that was thirty thousand... altogether that's a lot of bloody money."

I didn't think I would ever get my head around the fact that my partner was rich. I was used to minimum wage, and surviving on noodles when I didn't get enough weekly hours at my old job. I wasn't used to being able to buy whatever I wanted without thinking of the financial consequences.

I used to work at my local supermarket, but when all the bullshit happened last year I missed too many days without a viable excuse and I got fired. I hated my job, but it paid the rent. I know I didn't have to worry about paying rent now that Alec bought us a house, even if he did put my name on the deed too. I still wanted to earn my own income. I didn't want to rely on him for my finances.

Hopefully my writing would become more than a passion and turn into a full-time job. God knows I needed it.

"Did you tell him how you feel about him spendin' so much money?" Aideen asked as she sat on my sofa, behind me.

I turned to face her. "No." I frowned. "It's his money, I can't tell him what to do with it."

Aideen nodded in understanding. "I think you should ease him into the conversation. Just explain what life was like before he came along. Your uncle is loaded, and so is your ma, and you wouldn't take a penny from either of them. He can't expect it to be different with him just because you're both together."

You would be surprised.

"He thinks a lot of things now that we're together... He went out and bought us a house without me knowledge and he thought that was a good idea. He isn't aware of things right in front of him."

"You don't want to move out?" Aideen asked, her eyes wide.

I didn't know how to respond so I dodged the question and said, "He never even asked me, he just went out and bought the bloody thing. We're perfectly fine here. I don't see why he wants to keep changin' things when I'm still gettin' used to *him* being in me life."

Aideen was silent for a few moments before she said, "You have got to tell him how you feel, Kay. You will be miserable if you don't."

I knew that, I lay awake at night sick with the thoughts of it, but I couldn't say a word to him.

I wouldn't.

"He is so happy about movin' into the new house and to be movin' forward with our relationship... I don't want to ruin that for him."

Aideen furrowed her eyebrows at me when I looked back up at her and locked onto her concerned gaze. "If you don't level with him, eventually there won't be a relationship left to ruin," she said, her voice stern.

I was motionless as I sat before Aideen and stared at her with unblinking eyes.

"I don't mean to be harsh," she started. "But how long do you think it will be before you start to resent Alec for leadin' your life for you?"

I didn't speak, I just sat on the floor and stared.

"You're an independent woman, Kay, and you like being one. I love Alec, I do, but if he doesn't stop decidin' everythin' for the both of you he will lose you."

I was surprised when my eyes welled up and hot tears fell from my eyes and splashed onto my cheeks when I blinked. I quickly reached up and wiped the tears away, but it was too late, Aideen saw and was on the floor in front of me reaching her arms out and comforting me with a hug.

"How long have you been feelin' like this?" she asked me.

I wrapped my arms around her waist and dropped my head to her shoulder. "A good while," I admitted.

Aideen sighed as she swayed us from side to side for a few moments.

"I'm havin' nightmares too," I whispered.

Aideen froze, then after a moment she pulled back from me and stared at me with sad eyes.

She swallowed. "What are they about?"

I sniffled, "Everythin'. Darkness. The Bahamas. Storm gettin' hurt. Just... everythin'."

I burst into an uncontrollable sob and it must have shocked Aideen who flinched. She regained her composure and quickly pulled me back into a hug. She swayed and hushed me until my sobs became mere sniffles and my eyes ran dry.

"You need to talk to someone, Kay," Aideen whispered.

I gripped onto her tightly. "I am. I'm talkin' to you."

Aideen sighed and gave me a tight squeeze.

She said nothing further and I was grateful for it because if she said anything else there was a strong chance I would have gone into detail and told her everything that was going on inside my head. I couldn't let that happen, no good would come from releasing those demons.

It had been thirteen months since I left Darkness and all those horrible people behind me, and as far as anyone could tell I was fine. I appeared fine because I had myself in check, but Aideen saw a glimpse of how fucked up I really was about my past. Now that she knew I had nightmares she would push it until I told her everything. It was bad enough I told her about Alec because now she wouldn't rest until I spoke to him about how I was feeling.

"I'm fine," I said and cleared my throat.

I forced myself to breathe so I would calm down and stop sniffling, and when the tears stopped I pulled back from Aideen and gave her a small smile. I could tell she wasn't buying it though.

"I'm pissed that you have been strugglin' with this for awhile and you're only now tellin' me what's wrong. Your mental health is important, unload everythin' onto me if it'll make you feel better," she pressed.

KEELA

I waved her off. "We can talk soon, I promise... I just want today to go by without thinkin' about all the crap that's built up in me head. Okay?"

Aideen wasn't happy but she nodded her head anyway.

"Thank you," I said and gripped onto her hands.

She gave my hand a squeeze then said, "Wait, you're cool with gettin' married still though, right?"

I remained silent and Aideen gasped.

"You aren't?"

I shrugged my shoulders. "I don't know."

"Are you gettin' cold feet?"

"No, I'm just sayin' that marriage could be different than datin'. I mean who is to know what could happen? Disney never did a follow up on Cinderella—like, what happened after the shoe fit? Did they get on? Did they get divorced? We'll never know."

"Keela... are you really worried your future marriage to Alec could go south because you don't know how Cinderella and her lad ended up after they got married?"

Was I?

"I don't know," I admitted.

"I do. They lived happily ever after, it says so in the end credits of the film."

I rolled my eyes. "You're a very strange person."

"Says the woman who just compared a Disney film to her future marriage."

Oh God, she was right.

I groaned, "Maybe I'm losin' me mind."

Aideen snorted, "You lost it long ago, sweetheart."

I sat up and glared at Aideen. "You aren't helpin' me, you know?"

"I was just your shoulder to cry on, I've helped plenty."

I laughed. "I need your help, not emotionally though. Physically."

"You mean you didn't call me here to unload on me? Then why

did you call me?" she asked.

I was grateful she was changing the topic.

"I need your help to start packin'. We're movin' today and I've done nothin'. Literally nothin'," I groaned. "I was writing so well the past two weeks that I put it off and now it's movin' day and we're aren't movin' ready."

Aideen blinked her eyes. "You want me to *pack?*"

Did she listen to a single word I just said?

"Yes, I want you to help me pack!" I stated.

"Pack up your apartment? I thought you needed 'help'," Aideen said whilst using her fingers as air quotes around the word help.

"Why the air quotes?" I asked, bemused.

Aideen huffed and lowered her arms. "Because I thought you meant the *alcohol* kind of help, especially after what you just told me. I kind of assumed it would be the *hard stuff* kind of help."

I stared at my best friend and for the billionth time wondered why I continued our weirder than weird friendship.

"Alcohol kind of help?"

"Yeah." Aideen grinned. "You know, I help you get drunk."

I shook my head.

How this fool was employed as an educator to children I would never know.

"It's half ten in the mornin'."

Aideen shrugged. "It's five o'clock somewhere."

"There's somethin' wrong with you."

Aideen groaned. "Don't judge me, term started back on Monday and the kids are drivin' me insane already."

I raised my eyebrows. "You teach *second* class kids, they're all cuties."

Aideen growled, "Those eight year olds can be animals, do you hear me? Animals! I caught two boys forcin' another boy to eat fuckin' glue while givin' him a wedgie yesterday. They're evil, I'm tellin' you."

I laughed. "Find a career that doesn't involve kids then."

"No!" Aideen gasped. "The angels outweigh the devil spawn ten to one. Besides, I like imparting wisdom on the next generation."

Wisdom. Ha.

Those poor kids were destined to jobs as strippers and drug dealers as long as they remained under Aideen's care.

"I know you're thinking something bitchy, so I'm gonna say fuck you before I forget."

I snorted. "You're the strangest person I know."

"You pronounced coolest wrong," Aideen teased.

This girl!

I couldn't help but laugh. "Can you be serious?" I smiled. "I need you."

Aideen exhaled loudly, "Fine, where do you want me?"

"Face down, arse up." I smirked.

Aideen burst into laughter and seconds later a bark rang from my bedroom.

"It's nice to hear you too, you fat—"

"Aideen!" I cut her off.

Aideen laughed. "I wasn't goin' to say anythin' bad to him."

Ha ha. Bullshit.

"Yeah," I laughed, "and I'm Beyoncé."

Aideen raised her eyebrow at me. "You don't have the arse to be Beyoncé."

"Then I'll get some of Bronagh's arse—she has enough to spare." I grinned.

Aideen cackled at the same time laughter started up outside my apartment door. A few seconds later someone knocked on the door. I got up and opened my door without looking through the peephole.

I knew who it was from the laugh.

"Hey, what're you two doin' here?" I asked and greeted Bronagh and Branna with a hug.

Bronagh fist bumped me and said, "Alec called us and said you needed help with packin' so here we are."

I leaned against my front door and smiled. "Thank you, you're both brilliant."

Branna rolled her neck onto her shoulders and said, "We know, now let's get to it."

Ready to work.

I liked it.

I chuckled and closed my door only to yank it back open when a thud sounded against it and something, or someone, yelped. I widened my eyes when Ryder Slater hunched over in front of me and groaned in pain. He was holding his forehead and hissing. I panicked and placed my hands on his back.

"I'm so sorry, Ry!" I gushed. "Are you okay?"

"He's fine," Branna stated, waving him off. "He already has a damaged brain, nothin' else will increase his stupidity by much."

Ryder straightened up to his full height and hissed at his woman, "Bite me."

Branna snapped her teeth at him making Bronagh and Aideen laugh.

"I'm fine, Keela, thanks for *your* concern," he said, glaring in Branna's direction.

Branna wasn't paying him any attention so Ryder strode over to her and wrapped his arms around her. He lifted her into the air and she yelped with surprise. Ryder proceeded to spin around in a circle then and Branna screamed.

"I'm sorry," she squealed. "Stop spinnin' me!"

I was terribly confused as to what was happening so I looked to Bronagh, my face quizzical enough to make her laugh.

"He does that when she is bein' bitchy for no reason," she explained.

He spun her around in a circle?

I blinked my eyes. "And it works?"

Bronagh nodded. "She gets motion sickness so it straightens her attitude out when he does it."

I shook my head. "They have a weird relationship."

Bronagh nodded her head. "Dominic just tells me to piss off if

I'm being bitchy to him."

I burst out laughing. "Alec won't tell me in so many words, he just glares at me a lot and broods in silence. His silence screams what he is feeling though."

Bronagh smiled. "That's our Alec, he wears his heart on his sleeve. Poor lad."

I snorted and looked back to Ryder who sat Branna's feet back on the ground and held onto her shoulders until she got her bearings and stopped swaying like she was about to fall over.

"Is the bitch gone?" he asked her.

Branna growled, "Just about."

Ryder snorted and kissed the crown of her head and hugged her to him. I saw a small smile quirk at the corner of Branna's mouth as she put her arms around Ryder and hugged him to her.

"Love you," she mumbled.

Ryder grinned. "I love you, too."

Things were silent for a moment until Aideen made a heaving sound.

"Puke. Could you both be any cuter?" she asked Ryder and Branna.

Branna grinned. "Yep, would you like a demonstration?"

Aideen scrunched up her face and shook her head. We all chuckled and then us girls jumped with fright when someone burst into my apartment.

"Morning!"

I swung around and pressed my hand against my chest where my heart was pounding away.

"Omigod!" I gasped.

Bronagh and Branna yelped, "Kane!"

"You fuckin' bastard!" Aideen bellowed then stormed over to Kane and thumped him right on the chest. "You frightened the bejesus out of me, Slater. Don't bloody do that!"

Kane looked down at Aideen then to his chest and lifted his hand to rub away the pain that radiated there thanks to Aideen. He smiled when she shoved at him trying to hurt him once more. He grabbed her arms, spun her around and pressed her back into his front. He still had ahold of her hand so for the moment; he had her pinned against him.

"Nice to see you too, Ado," he purred into her ear.

She growled, "Let. Go. Of. Me."

Kane chuckled but did as she asked.

Aideen spun around and gave him the finger before she moved and stood behind me. I wanted to chuckle at her—he could easily get her if he wanted to but she thought having me between them somehow made it impossible.

"I didn't mean to scare you, I thought you heard us coming up the hallway," Kane said and shrugged his shoulders apologetically.

I looked to the empty space behind him.

"Us?" I questioned.

Kane looked behind him and sighed, "Dominic?"

Nico popped his head around the doorframe and smiled. "Hi."

I snorted, "What are you doin' out there? Come in."

Nico stepped into my apartment and scratched behind his head. "I heard everyone scream so I waited until you all took your anger out on Kane for scaring you before I showed my face."

I laughed while Kane glared in Nico's direction.

"Thanks, *bro*."

Nico smiled. "Anytime."

I shook my head at the brothers then beamed. "You came to help us pack, too?"

Nico nodded his head. "Alec is parking the moving truck downstairs, he got a huge stack of boxes with the truck too which is cool."

That was lucky because I didn't even think of boxes to pack everything into.

Man, I was so unprepared for this.

Today was going to be a long day.

CHAPTER FOUR

"Oh, my God," I whispered as my stomach burst into butterflies. I dropped my duvet back onto my bed in shock. I came in here trying to get a start on packing but any thought of packing left my mind when I saw Alec.

His long hair was gone. He had a buzz cut on the sides of his head, but the top was longish and pushed to the back, but some strands hung down on his forehead. I *loved* his long hair, but this cut allowed his stunning face more viewing time.

"You don't like it?" Alec winced.

The fucking opposite.

"You look so hot that I have butterflies," I admitted.

Alec raised his eyebrows. "Really?"

I nodded my head. "Alec... seriously. You're unbelievably hot."

I had to sit down on my bed so I could take all of him in.

I slowly scanned his sculpted body from head to toe. He was dressed in black jeans, a white fitted t-shirt and a thick unbuttoned grey cardigan that I got him from River Island last week. He had on black Timberland boots and I could smell his aftershave from where

I was sat. It was effortlessly casual, but he made the look something to gush over.

It felt like the first time seeing him, and I couldn't believe how gorgeous he was.

I couldn't believe he was my *fiancé*!

"Are you going to cry?" Alec asked, then laughed.

The bastard.

I quickly covered my face with my hands and shook my head.

I *was* crying, and I was embarrassed because of it.

"Kitten," he chuckled.

I kept my hands on my face and shook my head, again. "Feck off."

I heard his muffled laughter, then his footsteps, before I felt his hands on my thighs.

"Look at me, my lovely," he murmured.

I dropped my hands and opened my eyes.

Oh, Christ.

He was even hotter up close.

"Why are you so stunnin'?" I asked.

Alec smirked. "Why are you only now noticing?"

I growled at his teasing.

"It's still me, I'm still your Alec," he said and brought his face closer to mine.

My Alec.

Mine.

"I'm so lucky," I whispered.

Alec scoffed. "Please. The reaction you just gave me is how I feel every time I look at you."

"Stop it!" I screeched and covered my face again.

Alec burst out laughing and grabbed at my fingers. "Give me your mouth."

I lowered my hands and let his mouth seek out mine.

I lifted my hands to his shoulders then slid them upwards. For a moment I was saddened when my hands brushed over the buzz cut, but my insides clenched when I gripped onto the longer part of his hair. It was nowhere near as long as before, but I could still knot my fingers in it and that was good enough for me.

I allowed myself to get lost in his kiss, and barely registered that I was now lying down, and Alec was on top of me, pressing me down into our mattress. I was so wrapped up in him that I also didn't hear our bedroom door open.

"What are you both—oh, for fuck's sake! Can you not wait until later?"

I pulled away from Alec's mouth and screeched.

I wasn't naked and neither was Alec, but I felt like we were because the moment was personal and intimate.

Alec pressed his forehead into the space of mattress next to my head.

"Kane," he growled. "Go. Away."

"No," Kane retorted. "You woke me up to help pack your shit, so leave your girl alone and come help."

Alec snarled, "I'll *kill* you if you don't walk away."

"And I'll sit on you if you don't leave this room," Kane snapped back.

I couldn't help it, I laughed.

"Later," Alec murmured in my ear then kissed my cheek.

I held onto his arms. "Promise?" I murmured back as he stood up and pulled me to my feet.

He growled down at me and angled his face to kiss me again, but Kane was there to put a stop to that too.

"Don't even *think* about it."

Alec whimpered, "I hate you so much."

I snorted.

He turned then and dove on Kane who yelped, "I'm *sick*! You can't hit me."

I cackled as I watched Alec bring Kane to the ground and pin him.

"You fat bastard!" Kane snapped. "Get off me!"

Alec slapped Kane's face and the look of shock on his face sent me into a fit of laughter.

"You... you slapped me," Kane said.

He blinked at Alec in disbelief.

"You cock blocked me," Alec replied. "Be happy it's nothing harder."

Kane continued to blink, then a fleeting moment later his shock evaporated and rage twisted his handsome face. I felt my jaw drop open when Kane lifted his hands to Alec's arms and flipped him off his body. Kane quickly rolled to the side and slammed Alec onto his back and got in his face.

"Hit me now," he growled.

I was stunned to silence.

"How did you do that?" I asked Kane, but he was too busy to answer me.

Alec grunted in Kane's hold. "You motherfucker... sick my ass."

I didn't intervene—they attacked each other at random all the time so I knew it was nothing serious. The first time Nico did it to Alec though I just about had a heart attack. I took off my shoe and threw it at Nico's head to stop him. The brothers still teased me about it to this day.

"Try to slap me again," Kane repeated.

Alec grunted, spewed curses then grunted some more.

"I can't!" he hissed.

"Exactly," Kane growled. "Remember that."

He got up off him, then got to his feet and pulled Alec up with him.

"You're a dick!" Alec said and brushed his clothes off.

Kane grinned at him. "I know, now come on."

They left the room shoving and cursing at one another and it made me smile.

I loved the bond the brothers had—it was beautiful.

It was odd, and sometimes scary with how intense it was, but beautiful none-the-less.

I shook my head as they walked out of the room then snorted as I walked over to my dresser and heard Kane shout at Alec to get away from me. He laughed at Kane and ran back into our room.

"I forgot to say hello to her, give me a second."

I melted.

He was too cute.

"Hello Alec," I chuckled.

He walked up behind me. "Hello, Kitten."

"How many boxes did you get with the van?" I asked.

He snorted and kissed the back of my head. "Nice to see you too, Kitten. I missed you as well."

Missed me?

He was gone for about an hour.

I rolled my eyes. "Hi, I missed you too... How many boxes did you get?"

Alec laughed and playfully smacked my behind. "Twenty. My brothers are folding them and taping them now. They gave them to me flat and because they were free I didn't wanna complain."

I smiled, but said nothing as I thought for the millionth time about moving.

"Hey," Alec murmured in my ear. "Is everything okay?"

No, not at all.

"Yeah... I'm just stressed with the move," I replied, playing it off like it was nothing.

Alec placed his hands on my arms and gently rubbed up and down. "Are you sure that's all?"

I nodded my head.

"Keela," Alec began. "Talk to me, what's wrong?"

Everything.

"Nothin', I'm fine," I assured him.

His silence spoke volumes, so I decided to give him a little piece of what I was thinking.

"I've just never moved into a house with another person before, especially not another person who is my fiancé. It's sinkin' in that we're for real. I was convinced for a long time that you wantin' me was some kind of fluke. I was expectin' you to realise that you could have anyone, so why settle for me? Then you'd up and walk out."

Alec turned me to face him and leaned his head down so he could press his forehead against mine. "I don't know what else I can do to make you realise you're it for me. I don't see anyone *but* you. You're my life, Keela. I wish you knew just how much I love you and how lucky I am that *you* picked *me*. You don't know how beautiful you are, and I hope you never realise it because if you do, you'll realise you can do better than my sorry ass, then you'll up and leave *me*."

Yeah, *right*.

"Stop it," I mumbled and tried to pull back.

"No," Alec stated firmly and held me still. "You *are* beautiful. You *are* perfect to me. You *are* my life. You are *never* going to convince me that I am worthy of you. Kitten, I love you so much it hurts. Please realise that."

Oh, Christ.

I was about to cry. Again.

I quickly lifted my hands to my face and covered it completely.

"I hate you!" I said then burst into tears.

I hated everything.

I had this unbelievably beautiful person both inside and out, and he wanted me by his side for life, yet here I was doubting whether or not we were moving too fast. I wanted to be with Alec for the rest of my life, I swear I did... so why the hell did everything we were doing feel like it was too fast?

Alec took my emotional state as a good sign and put his arms around me and cuddled me to him. He thought I was overwhelmed by his profession of love, and I was, but what he didn't realise was that I was close to breaking down and revealing what was really wrong with me.

"Cry baby," he murmured to me.

I lightly chuckled and pulled back. "I'm fine, it's just the stress of movin' that has me so teary."

Alec nodded his head and kissed my forehead. "Let's go get a start on boxing and speed this day up. What do you say?"

I forced a smile. "I say lead the way."

We went out into our sitting room and leaned against the wall and watched everyone. Kane and Aideen were arguing, big shock there—not. Nico and Bronagh were kissing, another big shock—not. And then there was Branna and Ryder who were on their phones, which wasn't a shock either because lately they favoured their phones rather than each other's company, which I thought was sad.

"What are you both givin' out about now?" I asked Aideen.

She huffed. "*He*," she glared at Kane, "said us girls will be useless at packin' and I'm fightin' against it."

I looked to Kane. "That's a bold statement."

"But a true one," he replied.

Alec and his brothers snorted.

I looked over my shoulder to Alec. "What are you laugin' at?"

"Kane," he replied.

I frowned. "You... *agree* with him?"

"Say no," Nico whispered.

I rolled my eyes at his Man Bible advice.

Alec snorted and ignored his brother. "Yeah, I agree with Kane. You four will be no help and you know it."

The audacity!

"We can bloody be of help and we will be!" I snapped.

"No," Alec laughed. "You won't."

I growled, "Do you wanna bet?"

"Yes," Alec grinned mischievously. "I do."

CHAPTER FIVE

"I didn't mean a *real* bet," I said, nervously.

Alec smirked. "I did."

I scoffed. "*Really*? You *do* remember what happened the last time we made a bet, don't you?"

Alec chuckled and moved away from me. "Yeah, I *won* said bet. I got balls deep in your sweetness if I remember correctly."

Alec's brothers fist bumped him, which caused me to shake my head. Why did men feel the need to congratulate each other about shagging another person?

I rolled my eyes. "And what happened *after* that?"

Alec frowned. "Hell."

"Exactly. Bad things happen to us when bets are involved."

Alec waved me off. "We aren't betting your pus—"

I put my fists up indicating we would thrown down if he said *that* word.

Alec stopped speaking mid-word to smile at my actions.

"Your *private parts* aren't the grand prize this time around." He winked. "I was thinking more along the lines of your culinary skills.

How does this sound? If me and my brothers load up our side of the truck first then I win and you cook dinner for a month at our new house."

I was hesitant.

I enjoyed cooking but only because Alec and myself took turns when it came to the kitchen, so I wasn't sure if accepting the bet was the right thing to do.

Was it worth the risk?

I looked over my shoulder when I felt a sharp poke on my backside.

"We got this," Branna murmured.

I turned around and folded my arms over my chest as I scanned my teammates if I accepted the bet. All three of them were short, I was the tallest at five foot eight inches and even that was nothing on the brothers' height.

I sighed. "They are bigger and stronger than us, even Kane, and he isn't at full health."

Bronagh snorted then motioned for me to move closer with her index finger.

When I did she whispered, "*Please*, strength and body mass have nothin' to do with it when they are distracted. Dominic is slow as hell when it comes to cleanin' when I'm in the room—he can't keep his eyes, or hands, off me arse. I can pack perfectly fine while he will be slowed down. I'll render him useless to Alec."

Aideen snapped her fingers. "Oh my God, I've an idea."

Angels began to sing from the Heavens at Aideen's declaration.

"There's a first time for everythin'." I shrugged.

Aideen shoved me and it made me, and the girls laugh.

"Go on then Watson, enlighten me with your plan."

Aideen smirked. "Accept the bet, then we use our bodies to make sure the only hard time that will be had is in the lads' boxer shorts."

That... that actually had promise.

"I love it," Branna beamed and bumped fists with Aideen.

I raised my eyebrow and smiled. "I never thought I'd say this, but good thinkin'."

Aideen bumped fists with me. "I'm much more than a pretty face with big tits, Sherlock."

I snorted then with a grin on my face as I turned back to Alec and his brothers, and found them eyeing our group suspiciously.

"I accept your bet, *but* I want a different prize if I win."

Nico stepped forward and nudged his brother. "Don't agree to anything she says."

"What? Why?" Alec asked, warily.

"Look at them," Nico said and flicked his eyes over each girl. "They're up to something, I can feel it in my bones."

Alec narrowed his eyes and looked at each of us. "He's right, you four *are* up to something."

I feigned innocence and batted my eyelashes. "I have *no* idea what you're talkin' about."

"Your pretty green eyes don't fool us, Keela," Ryder glared. "We're Slaters, we see right through female bullshit."

"Ha!" Bronagh and Branna said in unison then burst into giggles.

Ryder nervously swallowed, and looked unsure of himself. "Well... most of the time we do."

Kane reassuringly patted his eldest brother on the shoulder and trained his eyes on his forbidden fruit. "Don't you associate yourself with whatever those three have planned, Aideen."

"I wouldn't dream of it, Germinator."

Ha!

Kane snapped his fingers at Aideen. "My bullshit meter is off the charts, Collins."

Aideen didn't reply and Kane looked lost at her lack of retaliation.

"Why aren't you cussing at me or telling me off?" he asked warily.

Aideen yawned. "Because I'm puttin' me energy into helpin'

Keela win this bet. I can argue with you later."

"Is that a promise?" Kane asked, grinning.

Aideen smirked. "We'll see."

The sudden sexual tension in the room could be cut with an erect penis.

I shivered. "Stop flirtin'. I feel dirty just standin' between you both!"

Alec snapped his teeth at me. "I'll clean you up real nice, Kitten."

I pumped my eyebrows. "Or make me dirtier."

Alec's smirk never wavered and I found myself moving towards him until a pinch on my behind made me yelp in pain. I grabbed my arse with both of my hands and swung around.

I instantly glared at Aideen.

"Ado!" I snapped.

Aideen shrugged. "Shag him with your eyes later, we have a bet to win."

I held my tongue as I glared at her and turned back around.

"I accept the bet you propose Playboy, but will you accept a different prize for me if I win?"

All four brothers folded their arms over their chests in unison and it made me smile.

They were so different yet so alike at the same time.

"What's the prize if you win?" Alec asked.

I bit my lower lip then released it and said, "You have to give us a striptease in any get up of my choosin'."

"Woot!"

I ignored Aideen's cheers, Kane's glares at her, the brothers' amused expressions and Alec's horrified one.

"You want me to do *what*?" Alec asked, sounding like he had something caught in his throat.

I smiled. "Give me and the girls a striptease."

Alec set his jaw. "Keela Elizabeth Daley."

My full name.

Uh-oh.

He was mad.

I continued to smile. "Nico told me you've done it before, back in your escortin' days. He said you wore a hat, a thong and a tie."

"Ow!" Nico shouted when Alec turned and punched his arm.

"Hey, no violence. If I'm not allowed to smack people, neither are you lot," Bronagh stated from behind me.

Nico huffed and rubbed his arm as Alec turned back in my direction and refolded his arms across his chest.

"Pick a different—"

"No," I cut Alec off. "These are me conditions for the bet."

Alec's eye twitched in annoyance.

I smiled at him, and after a minute of intense glaring Kane got irritated.

"Just accept the damn conditions, we'll have our section of the truck packed long before the princesses even have their side half full."

Princesses?

Oh, dude, wrong thing to say.

"Did you just call me a princess? You listen to me, you sick bas—"

"Ado!" Bronagh's voice snapped. "Deep breaths. Nice, big, deep breaths. You don't *need* to hit him, you don't *want* to hit him."

Aideen growled. "I really do."

I looked down and tried not to laugh at the sight of Bronagh convincing someone not to hurt another person. That was the definition of irony if I ever saw one.

"Time's a wastin'," Branna sang. "Are you acceptin' the bet or not, Alec?"

Alec snorted. "Yeah, I accept and when I win, you're going to be cooking me three course dinners everyday for a whole month, Kitten."

Yeah, we'll see about that.

"May the odds be in your favour!" Aideen said and bowed to

the lads.

All four of them stared at her.

"What is this, The Packing Games? Four men versus women, the first team to pack their side of the truck with boxes survives?" Alec asked, his tone teasing.

Bronagh laughed and devilishly smirked. "That's *exactly* what this will be, big brother."

All four brothers stared at Bronagh then looked to me. I grinned and they looked to one another and swallowed. The lads were nervous because they didn't know what we were up to.

They *should* be nervous.

I inwardly cackled like the evil witch I was.

We were going to destroy them.

CHAPTER SIX

"Okay, divide into your teams and sort out jobs between everyone. We have the movin' van until five this evenin' so that means we have to be completely packed here and unpacked in the new house in six and a half hours. No room for error. Understood?"

Alec and his brothers saluted me, and so did Aideen, which she found hilarious.

I rolled my eyes. "Get your arses to work."

Storm barked at my tone and everyone laughed.

I reached down and scratched his ears. "You can be on our team if you want, buddy."

Ryder cleared his throat. "He's a male."

Was he just figuring that out?

"So?"

"So," Nico chimed in, "he is automatically drafted onto the *men's* team."

"That's a stupid technicality," I stated.

Alec smirked at me. "No, he is a male so therefore he is on the male's team."

I wanted to fight that, but Aideen tugged on my arm getting my attention.

"Let them have him, all the fat shite does is sleep, fart, and eat. He is hardly goin' to help the competition."

While I didn't agree with the name-calling, Storm didn't do much else other than the things Aideen just listed so I pulled back and agreed.

"Fine, Storm is on your team."

Alec whistled and Storm shot over to his side, which surprised Aideen.

"He can run?" she asked, her eyes wide with surprise.

I rolled my eyes.

"No fraternising with the enemy. You steer clear of the humans with tits and vaginas. You got that, buddy?"

Storm barked in response to Alec as if he was answering the question with a whopping yes.

I grunted, "Traitor."

The lads chuckled as they moved into the sitting room to decide who would pack what. The girls and I moved down the hallway and into my bedroom to do the same thing.

"Okay, we need them to carry out the likes of the sofa and the bed—"

"Forget both, they're stayin' here with the landlord," I said. "Alec already bought new ones, they arrived at the new house yesterday. They're bigger and better, he said."

Branna blinked. "He bought both without even consultin' you first?"

I shrugged my shoulders trying not to appear like it bothered me, even though it did.

Greatly.

"But what if the sofa doesn't go with the room? What if you want a different design or colour?" Branna asked, her voice firm.

I shrugged my shoulders again. "It's his money, he can buy what he wants."

Aideen sighed. "You really have to get over that. You're both engaged to be married. While the weddin' is probably a while off, you have to get used to what is his is yours and vice versa."

I didn't have to get used to it vice versa, Alec already lived with me.

Everything I was he owned.

"It's difficult for her," Bronagh chimed in. "I'm very picky about Dominic and what he spends even though it's his money. He blew three quarters of it on absolutely nothing since we started goin' out. Now he needs to work otherwise we're broke. Money doesn't last forever unless you have a steady income."

I high-fived Bronagh.

"Exactly, that is *exactly* what I've been sayin'."

"Thinkin'," Aideen corrected me. "You've been *thinkin'* it, not sayin' it."

I growled at her, "Because it will look bad if I tell him not to spend his own money."

"You're a couple, Kay." Branna frowned. "You need to discuss these things."

"And *other* things," Aideen muttered.

I shot her a warning look and she closed her mouth. The sisters exchanged glances but said nothing. I didn't want to speak about Alec and myself anymore—I wanted to focus on packing.

What I *really* wanted was for this day to be done and over with.

"Okay, packin'," I began. "Bronagh, you and Branna start in here on the bedroom, I'll take the kitchen, and Aideen can start on the sittin' room. If the lads start to pack on somethin' that will help fill up their side of the van first, distract them with whatever means necessary. I *really* don't want to cook for the next month."

We all put our hands in together like a team huddle and cheered then laughed at our ridiculousness.

"Would it be too obvious to the lads that I was tryin' to distract Dominic if I got naked and bent over in front of him?"

I looked to Bronagh and just stared at her until she laughed.

"I'm jokin', but if I *did* get naked, Dominic would be completely taken out of the equation and that'd mean one brother down, three to go. The odds would tip even further in our favour."

I thought on it for a moment then shook my head. "You aren't gettin' naked, we will win this clean and fair."

Aideen nudged me. "How fair is what we're doin'?"

"Pretty fair, I mean we aren't doin' much. It's not our fault if the lads' dicks decide to pay attention to us."

Branna snorted. "Lets just do this before they think we have some huge conspiracy goin' on."

I smiled then turned and headed out of my bedroom and into the kitchen. I glanced to Alec who was playing on the floor with Storm. I inwardly smiled, using Storm to distract him never even occurred to me.

"Excuse me," I said and stepped over Alec and Storm.

I had a dress on so I made a point of stepping over Alec's head just so he could see up my dress.

"Keela!" he hissed and struggled to move Storm off his body as he got to his feet.

I jumped when Alec's arms slid around my back and his hands interlocked at my belly button.

"We're at war right now, sweetie. Hands *off* the merchandise," I said, sweetly.

Alec growled as he placed his mouth next to my ear, "You have no panties on."

I cringed.

God, I *hated* that fucking word, but I wouldn't correct him on it because I wanted my knickers, or rather my *lack* of knickers, to imprint on his mind.

"I don't? Huh. I must have forgotten to put some on—"

"Bullshit."

I fought off a smile.

"I'm sorry?" I asked, innocently.

"You heard me, bullshit. You don't just *forget* to put panties on. You have a fucking routine you follow when you get dressed—panties, bra, socks, then the rest of your clothes."

Did he pay attention to everything I did?

"That's true, but everythin' is a little bit hectic today. I can't go put some on now because the girls are in our room and it would be too obvious. I can't even grab a pair and slip them on somewhere else because Ryder is in the bathroom packing up our toiletries and I don't think you'd appreciate your brothers watchin' me shimmy on a pair of knickers in front of them in here."

Alec's hold on me tightened. "Damn right I wouldn't."

I devilishly smiled. "Exactly, so let me go and get back to packin'."

Alec growled when I moved away from him.

"How can I focus on packing boxes when I know you have no panties on under that dress?"

He wouldn't be able to focus, and that was exactly what I was counting on when I decided to take them off.

"I'm sure you will figure somethin' out."

I felt Alec's eyes on me as I opened a cabinet above my head and reached up for the plates and cups. I could feel my dress rise up my thighs as I stretched.

"God fucking damn it. Ryder! Switch with me!"

I glanced over my shoulder and watched as Alec stormed out of the room and down the hallway to the bathroom. I smirked.

Did he think he could get away from me that easily?

He was going insane if he thought so.

"Good idea, babe. Aideen, you take over the kitchen," I shouted. "I'll get my things packed in the bathroom in case Alec throws out the toiletries I like."

"On it!" Aideen shouted.

I briskly walked into the bathroom after Alec who tried to stop me from entering the room but groaned when I ducked under him and gained access anyway. I smirked to myself.

"Baby, close the door but not all the way, I need to get my towel rack from the top of the door."

Alec wouldn't look at me, but he did as I asked.

"Thank you," I chirped.

I stood on the side of my bath and pretended to lose my balance a little.

"Keela!" Alec shouted then jumped for me, opening his arms just as I fell into them.

I gasped, "Nice catch."

I leaned up and pecked the side of Alec's mouth and he growled.

"Just... just be careful, okay?" he murmured, his tough exterior fading for a moment.

I nodded my head. "I will, big boy. Don't worry about me."

Alec muttered something to himself.

I was so obvious with what I was trying to do, but Alec was concentrating so hard on *not* looking at me that he couldn't see how much I wanted him *to* look at me.

I glared at him through the mirror.

Apparently showing some skin wasn't enough—I had to turn things up a notch.

I turned and looked down to the bin next to the toilet.

"I thought I told you to clean this out?" I asked and bent forward.

"Clean what—Oh, Jesus."

I smiled to myself.

I felt cool air wash over my behind and I knew I was exposed.

Extremely exposed.

I jumped when Alec's hand gripped onto my arse.

"Alec!" I gasped.

He pushed me up against the bathroom counter.

"I can't. I can't *not* fuck you right now."

I looked through the mirror at him as he fumbled with the buttons on his jeans and frantically pushed them and his underwear down to his thighs. He was so flustered they didn't even make it all the way down his legs.

Looks like turning it up a notch meant I was using sex against Alec in my ploy to win this bet. He would kill me if he found out.

"Are you wet?" Alec asked me.

I didn't want to say no, but I wasn't.

I wasn't eighteen anymore—an arse grab didn't get me going.

"No, but you can still—Alec!"

Alec dropped to his knees behind me.

He might have disappeared from my sight, but I didn't need to see him to know what he was doing. I just had to feel him, and feel him is exactly what I did.

I balled my hands into fists when he put his tongue on me and plunged it into my body as far as it could possibly go. I focused on my breathing but whimpered when Alec moved from my entrance straight to my clit where he lapped and sucked at me like I was his favourite thing to eat.

Which I was.

"Yes," I groaned as an aching pulse built up and tormented me as Alec ate at me.

I opened my legs wider and pushed back into Alec's face.

His hands slammed down onto the globes of my arse before he squeezed them.

It hurt so good that I growled.

"Now," I pleaded. "Inside me. Now."

Alec tore his mouth away from my clit and stood up.

"Are you sure you want this in here?" he asked.

I didn't verbally reply, I couldn't.

"Keelaaaaaa," he hissed as I pushed my behind backwards and in one fluid motion he slid inside of me.

That was my answer.

Alec's hands instantly latched onto my hips and he thrust forward.

I gripped onto the faucets in front of me and held on tightly as I pushed back and met Alec thrust for thrust. I hushed Alec when the noise of the girls and lads arguing outside sounded. The bathroom door wasn't locked so if one of them opened the door they would get a nice view of what Alec and I were doing.

We were already playing dirty by using our bodies against the lads, but I didn't want them to know I stooped even lower by using sex against my man. They wouldn't judge me, but still, it felt like I was upping the ante by initiating sex in the first place.

"Nice and slow, Alec," I murmured. "We have to be quiet."

Alec growled and thrust into me harder causing me to groan out loud as pleasure shot up and down my body.

"Look at me."

I looked up into our bathroom mirror and made eye contact with him. I swear that watching his body move against mine was the sexiest thing I have ever seen. I didn't know why, but we never had sex like this before. I watched him fuck me when we were facing one another, but we never used a mirror to watch as he took me from behind.

Not until today.

"Oh, God," I groaned.

Alec leaned forward and kissed my shoulder before biting it.

I growled.

I loved when he bit and pinched me.

It really got me going.

We were silent as we gazed at one another in the mirror—my eyes involuntarily closed a few times when the pleasure became incredible. I bit down on my lower lip when Alec reached around and fingered my clit.

Don't think about it. Don't think about—Oh, Christ.

"I'm gonna come, I'm gonna come. Don't stop!" I hissed then pushed back against Alec as hard and fast as I could, giving my body exactly what it sought out, what only he could give me.

"I love you," Alec murmured then pinched my clit.

It sent me over the edge and head first into ecstasy. I slapped my hand over my mouth as wave after wave of glorious pleasure slammed into me. I momentarily stopped breathing, but when shivers ran up and down my spine I gasped.

Loudly.

Alec's movements slowed to pelvic twitches as he finished inside of me. I wanted to smile, but I jumped with fright and opened my eyes when I heard a loud whooping cheer coming from somewhere in the apartment.

"Alec, pull out! Don't let her use her pussy against you—Ow! Damn, Branna, I expect that from Bronagh, not you," Nico's voice whined.

I placed my forehead against the marble counter of my bathroom and groaned.

They knew what we were doing.

"I'm mortified."

Alec slapped my arse as he slid free from my body.

"Hearing us isn't so bad. They've walked in on us having sex plenty of times—"

"Not all at the same time!" I cut Alec off.

I stood up and turned to face him as he wiped himself with a wet wipe then dropped it into the toilet and pulled his jeans up, buttoning them closed.

"I *told* you to stop bending over."

I rolled my eyes. "I thought you were messin' with me."

I didn't think anything of the sort. I knew good and well he would crack if I bent over far enough.

"You have no panties on... I saw your pussy.... How much control do think I have?" he asked, annoyed.

None.

Absolutely none.

I couldn't help but giggle, and after a moment Alec lost his attitude and grinned then shook his head at me. He reached out for me and pulled me against him, hugging me tightly.

"I like watching you come like that, it's hot as hell."

I smiled as he kissed the crown of my head.

"I liked it, too," I mumbled and snuggled against his chest.

I groaned and moved away from Alec when I felt the act of our sex drip down onto my leg.

"This is the nasty part," I muttered and grabbed a few wet wipes so I could clean myself up.

Alec snorted and went about stacking up toiletries onto the bathroom counter while I used the toilet. Mid-way through relieving myself I looked up at him and snorted.

He glanced at me. "What?"

I shook my head as I reached for a roll of tissue.

"I never thought I'd go to the toilet in front of a man like it was nothin'."

Alec snorted, "It *is* nothing."

He went back to stacking shampoos and such while I swallowed when a thought entered my mind.

We were already acting like a married couple.

I refused to do this right now. I had enough on my mind with the move and the stress that it brought. I couldn't worry about how Alec and myself were acting. I wouldn't.

"Hey, what's that look for?" Alec asked me, jarring me from my thoughts.

I stood up and flushed the toilet, smiling as I moved to the sink so I could wash my hands.

"Nothing, just wonderin' how much shite we're goin' to get when we go outside."

Alec regarded me for a moment then chuckled. "It'll be fine, my brothers will keep the taunting to a minimum. I'll kick their asses otherwise... Can't speak for the girls though."

I snorted. "They'll high-five me."

Whoops.

"Why?" Alec asked, his eyebrow raised.

I smirked. "Because I got some in a bathroom."

Alec watched me for a moment then shook his head. "Women."

I laughed and began to re-fold the towels that Alec took off the towel rack and out of the small cupboard next to the mirror on the wall. When that was done, I re-organised the towels he'd just stacked. I threw out the half empty bottles of products and kept only the full and unopened ones. I explained I didn't want any of the opened bottles to open and spill in the van. The new ones had seals on them so they wouldn't cause any damage if they tipped over inside the van.

Alec nodded his head then opened the door when I had everything organised. I asked him to go get me two boxes and he was on his way out the door to do so, but froze at the last second. I swallowed when he turned to face me. I was sure he figured out what I did from the look he was giving me, but I relaxed when he said, "Those boxes are mine."

I rolled my eyes. "No, they're mine."

Alec stood his ground. "I stacked them *all* on that counter."

I placed my hands on my hips. "I re-stacked them and re-folded the towels. I also threw out the rubbish you wanted to keep. They're part of *my* haul."

Alec glared at me. "I'm not letting you past me with a single item from that pile."

Oh, really?

"Don't make me hurt you, because I will," I threatened.

Alec snorted. "What are you going to do? Jump up to try and slap me."

Dickhead!

"Don't be makin' fun of me height. I'm tall for a girl, *you're* the one who is freakishly lanky!"

Alec's laughter ticked me off so I decided to use other options to get him out of my way.

"Bronagh!" I shouted.

Alec froze.

"Yeah?" she called out.

"Alec said you should be have been cast in *The Hobbit*!"

Alec gasped. "You evil bitch!"

Seconds later a wild Bronagh appeared and jumped on Alec from behind.

"*The Hobbit?*" she growled. "I'll show you a hobbit!"

Alec screamed and reached up to his ears, the ears Bronagh had in her vice like grip.

I laughed as she pulled and steered him away from the bathroom and down the hall where he stumbled into our bedroom and onto our bed from the sound of Bronagh's cheer.

She was twisted.

She even said 'weeeeeee' at one point.

I was about to exit the bathroom but halted when Nico ran by me. "Let him go... Damn it, Bronagh, you're going to undo months of anger management classes. I'll tickle you if you don't let him go. Stop! You'll pull his ears off!"

I snorted as I casually walked out of the bathroom and grabbed two empty boxes from the stack of boxes next to the front door. I whistled as I walked back into the bathroom and carefully placed the towels and toilet rolls into one box, then everything else into the other box.

"Aideen, have you got a marker and tape?" I shouted.

Aideen came into the bathroom armed with both.

We wrapped up the boxes then marked 'Bathroom' on both boxes as well as my name just so Alec couldn't try and pawn them off as being his later. Aideen picked up the box of towels and tissues while I grabbed the heavier box. We both exited the bathroom then walked out of my apartment and down the stairs until we were outside the apartment complex. I picked the right side of the moving van as the side where I wanted all my boxes to go.

Alec could have the left side.

"Two down. God knows how many more to go," Aideen commented and wiped sweat off her brow.

I snorted and tied my hair up into a bun on top of my head. "So far so good."

Aideen chuckled as we walked side-by-side back into my

apartment complex.

"Using sex against the big lad was genius."

I cackled, "Right? Worked like a charm. How is disarmin' the other lads goin'?"

Aideen burst into laughter. "Dominic is strugglin', Ryder is tryin' his hardest to avoid Branna, and Kane doesn't understand any of what's happenin'. He is so confused by me sudden behaviour, but hasn't mentioned a word since I grazed my arse against him. You should have seen his face, it was like a virgin lad touchin' his first boob. He was all wide eyed and freaked out."

I was in tears of laughter by the time we walked up the stairs to my floor.

I bumped fists with Aideen and said, "Let's keep it up."

"You got it, boss." Aideen winked.

The wide smile that was on my face dropped when Alec bellowed out my name from inside our apartment.

"KEELA!"

Uh-oh.

I swallowed and looked to a grinning Aideen.

"I'm in trouble."

CHAPTER SEVEN

"Yes, baby?" I sweetly called out as I stepped inside my domain.

I looked to my right as Alec stormed down the hallway holding onto his ears. I looked past him and saw Nico pinning Bronagh down on my bed with one arm while he used the other to tickle her.

Poor lass, she was taking one for the team.

"Don't you 'Yes baby' me!" Alec snarled as he came to a stop in front of me. "You cheated me out of—"

"I didn't cheat you out of anythin', you abandoned your post so the bathroom items were fair game," I cut Alec off and strolled by him as I walked into the kitchen.

Ryder and Branna were in there. She was on all fours cleaning out my lower presses, and Ryder was standing behind her just watching. From the look of things he wanted to do anything but pack right at that moment. I forgot about Ryder and Branna when my love grabbed my arm and spun me to face him. I held onto Alec's arms so I wouldn't fall because I got a tiny bit dizzy from his sudden move.

Alec glared down at me. "You set Bronagh on me so you could smuggle my boxes out of the apartment!"

Smuggle. Ha!

"Oh, get over it you big baby," I said and chuckled.

Alec continued to glare at me as he said, "Fine."

I snorted, "Fine."

"*Fine.*"

Alec turned and stormed out of the kitchen while I watched him go with a smile on my face.

He was too easy to wind up.

"Trouble in paradise?"

I turned to face Ryder who spoke to me.

I shook my head. "Nope."

Ryder snorted as he glanced back at Branna, who was still on her hands and knees, and sighed. "I'm going to pack in the living room instead," he mumbled

He walked into the sitting room, but couldn't escape Branna because she was hot on his heels and it made me snicker. The lads truly didn't stand a chance.

I got to work on clearing out the kitchen. Thirty minutes passed by before I knew it and I had all the contents of the kitchen presses packed into four large boxes. Two of the boxes consisted of our large pots and pans, and the other two were filled with all the smaller items like cups, bowls, plates and the mountain of cutlery we had.

"Aideen?" I shouted.

Aideen entered the kitchen from the hallway and glanced at my boxes. "Nice."

I grinned and got to work at taping them closed and writing my name on the boxes then the contents because I forgot to do it while they were flattened. We called Branna and Bronagh in and we each carried a box down to the moving van. We loaded the boxes on my side, which brought the total to six.

When we were out of the van and standing on the path I turned to the girls.

"Status report?"

Bronagh grinned. "We've got the kitchen and the bathroom done. I'm nearly finished with the bedroom and Branna is gettin' there with the sittin' room."

I looked to Alec's empty side of the van and looked back to the girls. "Well... the plan is workin', they haven't got a single box packed yet."

We all high-fived one another and laughed as we re-entered the building and headed back up to my apartment. We cut the laughter and stayed silent as we entered my building. I froze slightly when I entered the kitchen and found all the lads sitting down and glaring at us.

Every single one of us.

Shite.

"What's with you lot?" I asked.

Alec growled at me, "Like you don't know."

Oh, bollocks.

"I've no clue," I said, feigning innocence.

Nico scoffed. "Cut the crap, we're onto you four."

Us girls shared a look then in unison we said, "What did we do?"

"That was creepy," Ryder mumbled.

Kane ignored his brother and said, "You're seducing us."

We all scratched our necks.

"That is ridiculous," I said, waving Kane off.

"No," Nico snarled, "It's not. I *know* you Bronagh. You're constantly touching me, bending over in front of me and drawing as much attention to your ass and body as possible. You know damn well what you're doing to me."

Bronagh remained silent, as did the rest of us.

"You seduced me in the bathroom, Keela," Alec hissed at me. "Then you stole my boxes right out from under me."

I wanted to laugh so I bowed my head and cast my eyes to the floor to avoid doing so. I glanced at Kane when he crossed his arms across his chest and stared at Aideen.

"You grazed your ass against me five times. Five. Times. You evil bitch."

I lifted my hand to my mouth and covered it when a snicker escaped.

"You think this is funny!" Ryder bellowed. "My cock was so hard for you Branna and you were all 'Stop it, we have to pack boxes.'"

I erupted into laughter at Ryder's impression of Branna, and so did the other girls.

"You four are unreal!" Nico shouted over our laughter.

I couldn't stop laughing, not even when Alec shot over to me and got into my personal space.

"This game you're playing stops now," he growled down at me.

I looked up at him, and smiled. "What game?"

"Don't pretend you don't know what we're talking about, we figured out what you four are doing."

I tilted my head to the side. "Which is what?"

We were going to quarrel over this—I could feel it.

"You're using your bodies to distract us so you four can pack and we can't," Alec stated.

My lip quirked. "No, we're not."

"Liar," Alec hissed.

The four lads then moved to the multiple boxes that were stacked over at the door. I frowned, and leaned over to look at them. I counted eight, and Alec's name was on them all.

"When did you do this?" I asked.

Alec smirked. "You four took ten minutes bringing your boxes downstairs. When we realised what you were doing to us and why, we knuckled down and speed-packed. It worked as you can tell."

Each lad grabbed two boxes and headed out of the apartment, not looking at us as they walked. I spun to face the girls.

"What the hell are we gonna do? They packed the entire fuckin' sittin' room!"

Bronagh sighed, "Relax, we still have the bedroom."

The four of us turned and walked down to my bedroom. I lead the way and opened the door then gasped when I entered the room and found five boxes stacked next to the doorway. Everything in the room was bare.

"How the fuck did they pack so fuckin' fast?" Branna snapped.

I looked to Storm who was lying on my bed and let out a whine. "Why didn't you stop them?"

"Because he is a lazy fat—"

"Not now, Aideen!" I cut her off with a growl.

She grunted and folded her arms across her chest. "He is on *their* team, remember? He is against us, just like those four fuckers downstairs."

I agreed with her as I glanced around my room.

"I'm gonna be stuck cookin' for an entire month!" I groaned.

This was bullshit.

"Alec sucks. Him and Dominic, and their stupid bleedin' bets," Branna huffed.

I agreed with that wholeheartedly.

"What if we just nick these boxes? What can Alec do?" Aideen asked.

"He can take them back."

We all screamed as Alec's voice spoke from behind us.

Male laughter erupted, and female growls were let loose.

"Don't do that!" Aideen shouted at Alec. "You just took ten years off me life."

Alec seemed pleased with himself then nodded his head to the right. "Step aside."

I stayed put. "Can't we at least talk about this—"

"Not a chance," Alec cut me off.

He was being so unreasonable.

"But Alec—"

"I said no, Keela," he cut me off again.

I screeched and balled my hands into fists.

"It's not fair!"

To become the toddler I was acting like, all I had to do was throw a tantrum.

"Not fair is distracting us for your own personal gain," Alec said as I stepped aside with the girls so he and his brothers could enter the room.

"You got somethin' out of it," I snapped.

Alec tensed as he picked up two boxes. "We'll talk about this later."

Wonderful.

"You're *so* gettin' spanked," Aideen murmured making the girls giggle.

Alec's lip quirked as he walked by me, and his brothers each sported their own knowing grin as they followed him, carrying boxes of their own.

Men!

I turned back to the girls. "Now what do I do?" I asked.

Aideen frowned. "Get the last of your things and... leave here."

My heart stilled and I took a step backwards. "So soon? But—"

"There is no reason to stay here, Kay. You're all packed up and ready for your new house with Alec."

Oh, shite.

"Right," I said and licked my suddenly dry lips.

Bronagh looked sullen as she said, "Are you okay?"

I nodded my head. "I'm fine."

Branna lightly smiled at me. "You're nervous."

Try terrified.

"Maybe a little," I murmured.

Branna chuckled. "You will be fine. Movin' out of here will be hard for you—it's been your home for the last few years, but your new house will be your home too, and Alec's. You will get used to it."

Will I?

"I hope so," I replied and sighed. "This sucks."

Bronagh was transfixed on watching me, her face contorted in a grimace.

"Are you sure that's all?" she asked.

I nodded my head. "Yeah."

She continued to stare at me, then she said, "You're lyin'."

I blinked. "What? No, I'm not."

"You are," she pressed. "I can see it. You're scared... but not just about movin' houses. It's somethin' more than that."

Aideen stepped to my side. "Drop it, Bronagh."

"No," she replied to Aideen without looking away from me. "We're your friends, and I want to know what is wrong so I can help you."

She was such a lovely person.

I forced a smile. "Bee, I'm fi—"

"Don't," Bronagh cut me off. "Don't lie to me, Keela. I *know* you're lyin'."

How?

I was silent for a long period of time, and during this time Bronagh, Branna, and Aideen just stared at me. Waiting.

"It's... It's just... I'm... I'm havin' nightmares. I'm rememberin' everythin' and I don't know if things are right with Alec. I just don't feel... right with meself," I blurted out then quickly looked out of my bedroom and down the hallway to make sure none of the lads were there to hear me.

I looked back from the hallway to the girls and found Branna was looking between Bronagh and myself.

"Why are you lookin' at us?" I asked.

Branna nudged Bronagh. "Tell her."

I blinked. "Tell me what?"

"I had them too... the nightmares."

Her admission took my breath away a little. "You did?" I whispered.

Bronagh nodded, her eyes filling with tears. "I had them for a long time. They still happen every now and then."

I swallowed. "Do you... do you see bad things?"

Bronagh nodded her head. "Yeah... I remember what I went through, but my mind adds my worries to my dreams and the bad things that I witnessed happen to Dominic or Branna, and I have to watch."

I gasped. "Me too! I see everyone—me uncle, Marco, and the brothers. A shadow figure kills Alec and I can't stop it no matter how hard I try, but the shadow figure turns out to be me and I tell myself I don't deserve Alec, and then the brothers ask why I let him die, and then I kill myself at the end of the dream, and then I wake up. It's the same one all the time. Some things differ, but it's always Alec who dies and I'm the one to kill him."

I didn't realise I was crying until all the girls stepped to me and placed their hands on me.

"It gets easier," Bronagh whispered to me and pulled me into a hug.

She rocked me as Branna asked, "Does Alec know?"

"No!" I gasped and pulled back from Bronagh's hold. "And he can't know. I don't want to worry him."

All the girls frowned at me, but I shook my head. "This stays between us—promise me."

Bronagh groaned.

"Bronagh, promise," I demanded.

She sighed, "I promise."

I nodded and looked to Branna and Aideen, and they both murmured, "I promise."

"Thank you," I said.

Bronagh sighed, again. "The part of your dream where you hurt Alec, is it because you're scared to lose him or somethin'?"

"Or that you're goin' to be the one to end it with him?" Aideen chimed in.

The Murphy sisters gasped. "*End it?*" they asked in unison.

"You don't want to be with Alec?" Bronagh asked, her eyes wide with shock.

I glared at Aideen who held her hands up. "It was a viable question."

I looked away from her and back to Bronagh. "I *do* want to be with him. I love him. I just don't know about how fast everythin' is movin' with us. It's so much for me to wrap me head around."

Branna blew out a sigh of relief. "So explain that to him, he will understand."

I frowned. "He won't, if he had his way we would be married and knee deep in babies."

"You don't want that?" Branna asked.

"I do, but not right now," I explained. "When he asked me to marry him we only knew each other just under two weeks. I fell for him too hard and too fast, I didn't think feelings could develop that quickly but they did and my acceptance to his proposal was fuelled on by almost losin' him to Marco and that entire fucked up situation. I was livin' in the now, when I should have been realistic and just started up a normal relationship and took it one day at a time."

The girls all listened to me as I spoke.

"So you just wanna be engaged for a few years?" Bronagh asked.

I nodded my head. "We're still learnin' new things about one another, and findin' out little things here and there about our pasts from before the Bahamas. I just want it to be me and him simply datin' for awhile longer... is that so terrible?"

All three girls shook their heads.

"No, it's not," Aideen said. "It's completely understandable."

Oh, thank God.

"You have to tell him eventually," Branna said after a moment.

I cast my gaze downwards. "I know, but I don't know how to go about it."

"You might wanna try today before we take all your stuff to the new house."

I froze. "I can't do that, he can't wait to move to the new house."

Bronagh look deflated. "Better you let him know your feelings here than when you move into the new house and can't come back here."

I thought on that for a moment and pushed the idea away. "No, I'm just extra touchy because of the move. Once we're settled into the new house I'll explain everythin' to him and we can go from there."

None of the girls looked happy with my decision, but they accepted it.

We all stopped talking and I quickly wiped away my tears when I heard laughter come from outside my apartment. Bronagh wiped her eyes too but, it was obvious from the redness and blotches on her cheeks that she had been crying. She was cursed with the evidence of crying—she couldn't hide it.

The lads entered the apartment and they called out to us. Alec spotted us still in the bedroom so they all walked down the hallway to us.

"I win, Kitten." Alec grinned. "I have more boxes packed than you."

I rolled my eyes. "Whatever. I'm gonna poison your food."

Alec laughed and looked from me to the girls. I saw the second his eyes landed on Bronagh and the change in his demeanour.

"Bee? What's wrong?" he asked, worry laced in his tone.

I smiled. They all loved Bronagh.

"Nothin'," Bronagh replied.

Nico stepped forward. "You were crying," he stated.

"I wasn't, I rubbed me eyes 'cause dust got in them... that's all."

She was the worst liar in the history of liars. She wouldn't look Dominic in the eye, and she kept glancing at me. Nico looked at me, and I cast my gaze down to my fingers and played with them. Bronagh was a shite liar, but I was pretty sure I was no better so I didn't look at him.

"What happened?" Nico asked us girls.

"Nothin'," I mumbled.

"Did you argue?" Nico asked us.

We shook our heads.

I glanced to the other brothers and found they were all staring at me.

I was startled.

"What?" I asked them.

Kane and Ryder remained silent, but Nico said, "Something happened, the girls keep looking at you."

Cheers, girls.

"Nothin' happened," Bronagh insisted. "We're cool."

"What were you four talking about while we were downstairs then?" Nico challenged.

Aideen snorted. "Ways to give Alec the shits if he makes Keela cook for him for a month."

"Hey!" Alec shouted. "You would have made me do a striptease if you won!"

I gasped. "I would have never—"

"Keela," Alec cut me off and gave me a knowing look.

I couldn't help but laugh. "Okay, I would have."

"Exactly."

We all chuckled then.

I glanced around. "What can I box that will even the game out?" I murmured.

"Nothing. Everything is done."

Damn it.

"I don't believe that," I said.

I went in search of anything that I could put into a box and pass off as an addition to my haul in the moving van downstairs, but I couldn't find anything. All of us girls were in the sitting room when the lads suddenly screamed and looked over at the front door.

"Storm!"

Storm?

"What?" I shouted. "What is it?"

Alec looked at me with wide eyes. "Storm ran out."

My baby!

He could get out of the apartment complex and run out onto the road and get hit by a car.

Oh my God!

I was going to vomit.

"Storm?" us girls screamed out in unison and ran out into the hallway of my building.

I jumped with fright when a bang sounded from behind us.

We each spun around and stared at my now closed apartment door.

What the hell?

I stepped forward and pressed down on the handle of my door, but it wouldn't open. It was locked, but it couldn't be, you had to lock it from the inside—

"Omigod!" I gasped and cut my own thoughts off.

I looked up and down the hall and gasped again.

"What?" Bronagh asked.

I kicked my apartment door. "They tricked us. We're locked out."

Bronagh was silent for a second before she exploded into rage. "You lyin' bastards!" she shouted and slapped on my apartment door.

Laughter sounded from inside my apartment. "All is fair in love and war, Pretty Girl."

Bronagh growled, "When I get me hands on you Dominic you're goin' to wish you were never born."

Nico laughed, "I'm not worried."

"You fuckin' should be!" Bronagh bellowed.

I could see Bronagh and how mad she was, Nico should have been scared.

Very scared.

"Ryder, open the door!" Branna asked politely.

"No can do, sweets," came Ryder's swift reply. "I'm only a man, I can't help finish packing with you seducing me."

"None of us can!" Alec shouted. "You all sunk to a new low, using our own cocks against us. You should be ashamed."

We should be ashamed?

"You used our love for an innocent dog to get us outside! You said he ran out!" I snapped.

Alec cackled. "That was your mistake."

"What was?" I growled.

"Believing Storm would willingly run anywhere."

All the lads burst into laughter.

"Bastards!" I yelled.

I angrily folded my arms across my chest and glared at the peephole of my door. I had a feeling like we were being watched so I gave the peephole the middle finger and more laughter sounded from inside.

"Your girl is pissed, bro," Kane said, then chuckled.

Aideen growled from my left, "You wait, Kane Slater. You just wait."

Kane howled with laughter. "What are you going to do, shout at me? I'm *so* terrified."

Aideen shook with anger, Bronagh and Branna shouted in annoyance, while I seethed in silence.

They were going to pay for this.

Big time.

CHAPTER EIGHT

"Are you not talking to me?" Alec asked as I angrily shoved my phone and its charger into my handbag.

I slung it over my shoulder and smacked Alec with it in the process.

"You're still pissed, I get it. No need to hit me," he said and took a step away from me.

No need to hit him. *Ha!*

I should kill the fucker for what he did.

He locked the girls and me out of my apartment so he and the lads could triple check that everything was packed up. He left us outside for twenty minutes while they searched. The dickheads. They even used Storm getting out of the apartment against us. They were evil, and I refused to look or speak to any of them.

When I packed up my handbag, I picked up my laptop case and put the strap over my shoulder. I looked around my bare apartment to make sure I had everything one last time before we left. My landlord would be by to check everything out in a few hours, and once everything was to his liking he would put my deposit on the apartment into my bank account.

I reached into my pocket and pulled out my keys, I took off the apartment key and placed it on the counter. I heard Alec brush his pockets, then his own keys jingled. He unhooked his key from the chain, and reached around me to place it on the counter next to mine.

I was going to cry.

The reality that I was moving really hit home, and I was saddened by it. I sniffled and seconds later, I felt hands slide around my waist from behind and a chin rest on my head.

"Don't be sad," Alec mumbled.

I was sad though.

Alec chuckled as he turned me to face him. I forgot what a fucker he was for the moment and put my arms around him. I hugged him tightly and repeated in my head that I was doing this for us. We needed the extra space—Storm couldn't handle this apartment anymore, and neither could Alec with his ever growing pile of crap—I mean belongings.

It was only a house move. I was still going to be in the same area, only in a nicer estate and in a nicer and bigger place. I would still see all my friends, and still be able to work perfectly fine... So why the hell did it upset me so much?

"Are you ready to go?" Alec asked me and kissed the crown of my head.

Am I ready?

No.

Will I ever be?

Probably not.

"Yeah," I whispered. "Let's go."

I pulled back from Alec and gripped onto his extended hand. We walked over to the door of the apartment and I turned around to look at everything once more. Alec gave my hand a squeeze and with a shaking hand I reached for the apartment door and stepped into the hallway, closing it after me. The lock clicked into place and I let out a little sob.

It was done.

We were moved out of my apartment... no, it wasn't mine anymore. It was just an old apartment now.

Holy crap.

I sucked in a deep breath and just as I was about to walk down the hallway with Alec, the doorway across the hall from us opened, and Mr. Pervert stepped out. He was holding an envelope and a bouquet of flowers.

"Hey Keela," he said and made a point of not looking at Alec. "I... I got you these flowers as a goodbye because I knew you're movin'."

I stared at the flowers then at Mr. Pervert, and burst into tears.

"Thank you," I said and stepped forward, throwing my arms around the man who creeped me out for years.

Maybe I was wrong about him, maybe he was—

"Hey, don't sniff her fucking hair. Bro, come on. I don't want to kick an old man's ass, but I will."

Scratch what I just said—Mr. Pervert was still creepy, but he was a *nice* creepy. I mean, he *did* buy me flowers. I stepped back away from Mr. Pervert as he deeply inhaled and I shivered in revulsion. I shook it off and leaned forward and took my flowers.

"Thank you." I smiled.

Mr. Pervert nodded and handed me a white envelope.

I raised my eyebrow. "The last time you gave me an envelope it changed me life."

Mr. Pervert blinked in confusion, but said, "It's just a farewell card."

I surprisingly chuckled. "Thank you, again. I love the flowers and the card, they're great."

Mr. Pervert perked up and Alec growled, "My woman, back off."

Oh, Christ.

Alec's, me Tarzan you Jane, attitude was back.

I ignored Alec and smiled to Mr. Pervert. "It was... lovely being your neighbour."

"It was wonderful being yours," he replied.

Gah.

"Bye." I smiled.

"Take care."

I turned and walked away then shook my head when Alec chose to walk behind me instead of beside me.

"Don't shake your head, if he wants an ass to stare at he will have to make do with mine."

I laughed as we headed out to the stairs and descended them.

"You're crazy," I said.

We left my apartment building and joined everyone else who was standing next to the moving van.

"Where the hell did you get *those*?" Bronagh asked me causing everyone's gaze to turn my way.

I grinned and proudly held up my flowers. "Mr. Pervert."

The lads all looked to Alec and laughed.

"How badly did you want to hit him?" Nico asked.

Alec growled, "I'm still contemplating going back inside and kicking his ass."

I rattled my head. "Relax, he was just being nice."

"Nice my ass," all four brothers said in unison, which cracked up the girls.

"They all share the same narrow mind," Aideen teased.

I fell into Alec and laughed.

"Ha. Ha. Ha. Shut up," Kane deadpanned making me laugh harder.

When the laughter subsided Aideen spoke up.

"Okay, Keela, me and you are goin' in your car. The girls are going with Ryder and Nico, and Alec is drivin' the movin' van while Kane is drivin' his SUV," she said, taking leadership. "Does that sound cool?"

I nodded my head. "Yep."

"Excellent. Let's get on this, bitch," she announced.

We all snorted.

Alec kissed my head. "We'll be right behind you."

I nodded my head and walked over to my car. I unlocked it so Aideen could get in then I opened the back door and laid my flowers on my back seat with my bags, then closed the door and got into the driver's seat.

"How are you doin'?" Aideen asked as I started the car.

I put the car in gear as I shrugged my shoulders. "I don't want to say anythin' positive because I'd be lyin'."

Aideen sighed as I pulled out of my car parking space for the last time.

"I think you're puttin' way too much thought into this. You can live in the newer, bigger, and way better house with Alec and just remain engaged. You don't have to plan a weddin', you don't have to do anythin' but enjoy one another."

I processed that thought.

I glanced at Aideen as I drove. "I never thought of it like that."

"Of course you didn't," she mumbled. "You were too busy seein' the horror in movin'. It's *not* a big deal. You can have what you want, just ten minutes away from the apartment complex."

I thought about it and realised Aideen was right. Moving was just stressing me out, but once it was done, it would be over and I could get to enjoying Alec at a leisurely pace.

"You have no idea how much better you made me feel," I breathed.

Aideen reached over and rubbed my shoulder. "I'm glad, I hate seein' you upset."

I lightly smiled. "I know, but the weight of me worry just faded away thanks to you."

Aideen was silent for a moment until she said, "Now we just have to deal with your nightmares."

My hands tensed around the steering wheel of my car. "Can we *not* talk about that, please?"

"Fine," Aideen reluctantly said, "but now that we know Bronagh is in the same boat as you, you *have* to talk to her."

"I will," I said firmly.

Satisfied, Aideen nodded her head once then turned and looked out the car window.

I already made a decision to speak to Bronagh about my nightmares back in my apartment. When she admitted she suffers from nightmares too, I felt... overwhelmed with relief. I was *so* relieved I wasn't on my own, and what went on in my head wasn't me losing my mind, but the effects of my past playing horrible tricks on it.

"I don't mean to bring this back up, but when are you goin' to tell Alec you don't wanna get married for a few years?" Aideen asked me.

My stomach churned at the thought.

I exhaled. "Whenever the time is right."

I had to wait until the perfect moment to unload this on Alec—he was a complex person and unless I worded things correctly he would take my feelings the wrong way and things could go horribly for us.

"I just need some time. I have to sort out me own head first," I murmured.

Aideen put her hand on my shoulder. "I've got your back."

I glanced to her and smiled.

Having friends like her got me through the tough times, hopefully the only times ahead for Alec and I are good times. God knows we could use more good times in our life. We've had a past full of bad ones.

CHAPTER NINE

"Can you believe the size of this place?" Aideen shouted from the kitchen of mine and Alec's new house.

Her voice echoed.

I chuckled as I placed a picture of Aideen and myself on the sitting room wall. I was perfectly fine on my little stepladder, but Alec was apparently afraid I would fall and hurt myself so he took it upon himself to stand behind me and hold onto my hips. His hands occasionally slipped though.

"That's me arse, Playboy," I said as I adjusted the frame on the wall.

Alec squeezed my behind. "And what a perfect ass it is."

I snorted. "Give it a rest."

Alec gave my arse one more squeeze, then slid his hands up to my hips.

"Is this straight?" I asked him.

He took a step back then to the left and observed the picture. "Yep."

"Great. One down, a million more to go."

Alec smiled wide.

Smiling was all he seemed to do since we arrived at our new house. We had been here with the gang the last three hours. It was sometime after five in the evening, and the majority of our boxes were completely unpacked. Having so many people to help out sped everything up, we all moved ten times faster.

Bronagh and Branna unboxed the bathroom boxes and put everything in the en-suite in mine and Alec's master bedroom. We'd have to buy more bathroom stuff though because each of the bedrooms had an en-suite, and then there was a bathroom on the bottom floor of the house for any guests who came to our house.

There was so much space that I didn't know what to do with myself.

I wasn't alone though. Storm had no idea what to do when Alec brought him inside. At first he tried to mark his territory, but Alec's shout kept the piss inside him. He then settled on rolling his body over every square inch of the floor, and walls, in each room. He rubbed himself all over the sitting room, the hallway, the kitchen, and the downstairs bathroom. Now he was sleeping in his bed in the kitchen, exhausted from his antics.

"Everything we brought with us is unpacked, and the place still looks empty."

Alec slapped my behind. "So go shopping."

I stepped down off the stepladder and turned to face him. "Don't say it like that, you know I'm broke."

Alec groaned, "Please don't start this again. My money is your money."

"But it's not. It's just *your* money," I argued.

Alec pinched the bridge of his nose. "We're engaged, we share things now."

"I don't care if we're married and have fifty kids, you *can't* convince me that all your wealth is now mine. I don't feel right about it. Just wait until I start earnin' money so I feel like I'm contributin', okay?"

Alec was staring at me. "Fifty kids, what the fuck do you think I am?"

I surprisingly burst out laughing and shoved Alec who was grinning at me.

"Fine, I understand what you mean. You want to contribute, and don't want to depend on me for everything."

I hugged him. "Yes, exactly."

Thank God he got it. Finally.

We got back to sorting our things out around the house. An hour later my phone rang as I was in the middle of pushing a cushion into its cover. I needed a break, my arms were hurting from the surprisingly difficult task.

"Hello?" I asked when I answered my phone.

"Well if it isn't my future sister-in-law."

A smile lit up my face as I said, "Damien!"

Damien's rich laughter flowed through the receiver of my phone and warmed my heart.

"How are you, Kay?" he asked.

I sat on the floor of my half empty sitting room and crisscrossed my legs, over one another. "I'm hangin' in there. It's movin' day for us, I'm in the new house."

Noise came from Damien's end of the phone then it went away as he cleared his throat. "Sorry, damn street races. What were you saying?"

I smiled. "I said I'm in the new house, it's movin' day."

Damien chuckled. "Is my big brother still alive?"

I gasped. "Of course, why wouldn't he be?"

"Because Alec doesn't take a lot of things seriously. I have a strong feeling he is making moving houses a bit more difficult for you."

He had no idea.

I snorted. "He actually hasn't been too bad. He won a bet so he is actually pretty happy and keeping to his own company."

"A bet?" Damien asked, a smile sounding through his tone.

"What were the terms?"

"Boys against girls, whoever packed up their sections and got the boxes into the moving van first, won. Us girls lost... but we went down fightin'." I smirked.

I imagined Damien shaking his head as he laughed.

"What did you and the girls do to try and prevent my brothers from winning?" he asked.

I blinked. "Why do you think we did somethin'—"

"Keela," Damien cut me off, his voice knowing.

I giggled. "We used our bodies to... *distract* them from completing their task before we completed ours. We were *very* successful."

Damien's laughter at the other end made me smile, but the gasp of horror behind me didn't go a miss.

"You cheating little bitch! I *knew* it!"

Uh-oh.

I looked over my shoulder and gnawed on my inner cheek when the pissed off form of my fiancé came into my line of vision.

"Hey baby." I innocently smiled.

"Don't you 'Hey baby' me. You cheated, Keela... and you lied about it!" Alec snapped as he stomped over and stood in front of me.

I had to lie back on the ground so I could look up at him without hurting my neck.

"It wasn't cheatin', not really. We didn't physically do anythin' to halt your process of packin', apart from us havin' sex, we just—"

"Got us so hard we couldn't see straight let alone pack fucking boxes."

That sounded about right.

"He sounds mad," Damien's voice whispered in my ear.

I snickered. "He *is* mad."

Alec reached down and snatched my phone away from my ear and out of my hand.

"Hey, that's rude!" I snapped and stretched my arms up high trying to reclaim my phone, to no avail.

Alec ignored me, and my slapping at his legs, and placed my

phone to his ear. "Who the fuck is this?"

Silence.

I watched as a smile stretched across Alec's face. "Baby brother! It's about damn time you called, you have Dominic worried sick!"

Silence.

I lifted my arms and placed my hands behind my head as I gazed up at Alec.

He frowned as Damien spoke. "Anything we need to worry about?" he asked.

I raised my eyebrows and looked at Alec expectantly, but the arsehole ignored me.

Alec released a breath. "So come home then, if you're bored over there why stay?"

I tilted my head to the side when Alec began to pace from left to right in front of me.

"How soon?" Alec asked then when Damien answered his face dropped.

"That could be years away, Dame."

I sat upright and got to my feet, then I stepped forward and wrapped my arms around Alec's waist and rested my head against his chest. Alec used his free hand to rub up and down my back.

"Yeah, I know, you've got shit to work through."

I hugged Alec tightly when he sighed and his body deflated.

I felt horrible for him.

He missed Damien—all the brothers did.

"Yeah, man, you got it," Alec said to Damien then chuckled. "You want to speak to her again?"

Alec nudged me and handed me my phone back when he got my attention.

I took the phone and placed it to my ear. "Hello again."

Damien chuckled. "You're driving him crazy, you realise that, don't you?"

I snorted. "I'm aware of it, yes."

Damien cackled through the phone and Alec vibrated with silent laughter because he heard it.

"How is your writing going?" Damien asked me.

I blushed. "It's fine."

"You talk to Dame about your writing, but not me?" Alec asked me, his tone annoyed.

I rolled my eyes. "You beta read the first ten chapters of me book and when you got to the sex scene you *laughed*!"

"Because no man moans that much during sex!" Alec laughed.

I glared at him. "*You* do!"

"Oh, burn!" Damien teased.

Alec glared at my phone, then at me.

"Go away while I talk to your brother," I said and walked over to our new sofa.

I sat down as Alec walked out of the room cursing to himself.

"I miss you guys," Damien sighed when his laughter subsided.

I frowned. "We miss you too. I'm dyin' to hug you. It sucks that we haven't met in person yet... you'd love me."

Damien laughed. "I already love you, spitfire."

I chuckled. "I love you, too. Aideen doesn't love you, but she fancies you. She said you could be her boy toy."

Damien snickered. "She's hot, I'll take whatever I can get."

I gasped. "I'm tellin' Kane!"

Damien whooped with laughter and it made me smile.

"I gotta go, babe. I have the early shift at work tonight."

I heard the sadness in his voice and it broke my heart—he was always sad.

"Okay, sweetheart. Stay safe, and call back soon."

"I will," Damien said. "Give everyone my love."

"You got it. Bye."

"Bye."

The line clicked as Damien hung up his phone and I frowned. I wished I could help him, but I had no idea the depth of his problems or what the hell it was that had him so down. Alec shone some light on his brother's past, but I'm sure not everything was told to me.

"Keela?" Alec's voice shouted from somewhere in the house.

"What?" I called back.

"I left my phone in the moving truck, will you come with me while I go and pick it up?"

That meant I could get out of cushion duty.

Sweet.

"Yes, let's go!"

CHAPTER TEN

We just left the building where Alec rented the moving van from, but they assured him there was no phone inside when he delivered the van back to them.

"I can't believe you lost your bloody phone," I grumbled as I climbed into Alec's SUV.

Alec got into the driver's seat and slammed his door shut. "I didn't lose it. Those bastard's clearly have it, which means they stole it from me!"

I shook my head as I buckled my seat belt.

"I don't know why you're giving me attitude either—if it was *your* phone you'd lose your shit," Alec stated as he started up the SUV.

I pressed my fingers against my temples.

I wasn't doing this, I wasn't arguing with him over a fucking mobile phone.

"Stop talkin'."

"No," Alec quipped. "You'd raise Hell if it was—"

"Shut. Up."

"—your stupid phone," Alec said, continuing on his rant like I didn't just speak.

"Alec. Stop."

He grunted. "I *just* bought that fucking phone too, and now it's gone."

Oh, my God.

He wouldn't close his mouth.

It was impossible for him to just shut the fuck up and it was grating on my nerves.

He was exasperating.

"Can you just stop?" I asked Alec whilst I rubbed my throbbing head. "I'm tired, we have been on the go since half ten this mornin'... I just want to go to bed and sleep for a week. The girls and I unpacked *everythin'* in the new house while you brought the movin' van back to the rental place. I'm knackered so just shut the fuck up. *Please.*"

Alec blinked at me. "Well... you're rude."

Rude?

He thought *that* was me being rude?

I said please!

"Honey, that was me being nice," I huffed then sighed. "I'm tired, Alec, don't you get that? I just want to drive home in silence and you refuse to stop speakin'."

Alec didn't reply.

He did what I wanted and remained quiet, but he did it with a silent attitude. I glanced at him out of the corner of my eye and caught him squeezing the steering wheel of the SUV a little too tightly. His posture was a little too straight for him to be relaxed, and his set jaw screamed he was mentally cursing me out.

All of this got on my already worn nerves.

"Why do you look like you're goin' to kill someone?" I asked him.

He growled. "You just told me to shut the fuck up, so that's what I'm doing."

I rolled my eyes. "Whatever."

"Whatever," Alec mimicked.

Bad move.

"Really? You want to start somethin' when I'm this tired? Try it and see how it pans out for you," I threatened.

Alec laughed. "What are you gonna do? Not put out. Oh, no, what ever will I do?"

Wanker.

"You can fuck *yourself*, that's exactly what you can do," I snarled and turned my body away from him.

Alec snorted to himself. "We'll see."

Excuse me?

"What's that supposed to mean?" I asked, my tone firm.

Alec shrugged his shoulders. "We'll see how long you not putting out will last—I give you until midnight."

Was he serious?

"I'm not a sex deprived maniac, I can *easily* go without shaggin' you without it botherin' me," I stated.

Alec laughed. "Yeah, right."

I could feel my temper rising.

"I'm serious, Alec. I don't need sex with you, I don't even need to sleep in the same bed as you," I said, my voice raw.

Alec continued to nod his head. "You keep telling yourself that."

I opened my mouth, but closed it because I was about to say something that I would regret later on. I was going to say I didn't need him at all, but that was a lie. I did need him, but not for the reasons he thought.

"You're so disrespectful. You want me as your wife, yet you treat me like a dog who can't go a day without humpin' your leg."

I turned my body and faced the window of the SUV as Alec drove.

"I don't mean it like that and you know it," Alec said, his voice a grumble.

I didn't reply.

I was tired, and I just wanted to go back to the new house and be on my own so I could sit and be in peace.

"Keela?" Alec murmured after a few minutes of silence.

Again, I didn't reply.

"I'm sorry," he said. "I didn't mean for you to take what I said in the way you did, I think of you as nothing but a blessing in my life. I love you."

Damn it.

"Say something."

I sighed. "I heard you, I just want to go back to the house and be on me own. I'm... I'm just tired."

"Tired of what?" Alec asked. "Me? The move? In general?"

"I'm tired of everythin'," I replied honestly and went back to looking out the window.

We drove the rest of the ten minutes back to the new house in silence. When we pulled up in the driveway I was confused, there was a black sports car parked in our driveway and I had no idea who it belonged to.

"Who is here?" I asked.

"I'm not sure," Alec replied, but he wouldn't look at me.

He got out of the SUV and I followed.

He waited for me to walk ahead of him before he fell in step behind me. I walked up to the door and tested the handle, but found it was locked.

"Do you have a key?" I asked Alec.

He leaned over me and inserted his key into the key slot.

"It's our house," he said and turned the key. "Of course I have a key, yours is in the kitchen."

I stepped forward and pushed the door open. We stepped inside and closed the door. I walked down the hallway and turned into the sitting room when deafening screaming erupted and figures of people jumped out at me. I jumped backward and screamed bloody murder.

"Surprise!" voices shouted.

Surprise?

What the fuck?

"It's okay," Alec's laughter came from behind me.

"What is this?" I asked him pressing my back into his front as I tried to back away from all the smiling faces.

There was only fifteen or so people in front of me—the brothers, the Murphy sisters and Aideen made up six of them. The others were faces I knew from Branna's job, and Dominic's friends from his gym.

Alec's mouth lowered to my ear. "It's a housewarming party."

A housewarming party?

"Are you fuckin' serious?" I asked and turned to face Alec.

He scratched his neck. "I didn't think you would be as tired as you are. I thought you would be excited for a party."

I stared at Alec unblinking for a moment then shook my head at him. "We aren't even fully moved in yet. There are boxes everywhere."

"We took care of the boxes," Bronagh's voice chirped from behind me.

I turned to face her. "The place is not fit for guests—"

"We made it fit for guests," Aideen cut me off, and grinned. "You need a drink. Don't argue with us."

I wanted to argue, I wanted throw everyone out on their arses and march straight up to bed, but I didn't want to be *that* woman, so I smiled.

"Thank you," I said to everyone.

I jolted when music started up and blared throughout the house.

"Where is that comin' from?" I leaned my head back and asked Alec.

Alec moved his mouth down to my ear and said, "Dominic brought his Beats Pill over from his place, it's pretty loud."

I'll say, the stupid thing could wake the dead with the volume of it.

Alec moved around me and greeted the faces smiling at us, so I followed suit and did the same. After I was done, I excused myself to go into the kitchen to get a glass of water. I'd just downed my glass when he spoke from behind me.

"How mad are you?"

I gritted my teeth. "I could fuckin' kill you right now."

"Trust me, if I knew you would have reacted like this I wouldn't have arranged it for you."

I turned to face Alec. "You arranged this for *me*? Don't you dare lie—you arranged this for *you*. This entire fuckin' move has been about you. This house? You. The SUV? You. The furniture? You. Everythin' else? Fuckin' *you*!"

I stormed forward and brushed by Alec but he caught my forearm and jolted me back to him.

"Ow!" I shouted. "You're hurtin' me! Let go!"

Alec kept his hold on me, but loosened it slightly. "What the hell is wrong with you? Why are you being like this?"

I tried to push Alec's hand off me but his grip was too tight. "I'm not being like anythin'... let me go!"

"No!" Alec snapped. "Talk to me."

That was the last thing I wanted to do.

"Dominic!" I screamed, using his full name to show I needed him.

Alec stared down at me with wide eyes. "Why the fuck are you calling him?"

Dominic shot out of the sitting room with Kane behind him, but when Kane saw it was me and Alec in the kitchen doorway, he closed the sitting room double doors and kept our guests inside with the music blaring.

"What's wrong?" Nico asked as he walked towards us.

I pulled my arm. "Tell him to let me go, he is *hurtin'* me."

Nico widened his eyes then looked to Alec's hold on me then to his brother's face. "Bro..."

"Don't, Dominic," Alec snarled. "Just... *don't*."

He let go of me and I quickly pushed away from him. I proceeded to run down the hallway and up the never-ending staircase, taking the stairs two at a time. When I reached the top of the stairs it took me a second to remember which door lead to our bedroom.

I hated that I was somewhere so unfamiliar, and I hated that Alec threw a stupid housewarming party.

My head was killing me, and the blaring music from downstairs did nothing to ease the pounding in my skull. I entered my bedroom and closed the door behind me. I walked over to our new bed and I was grateful there were sheets and covers already on it. I knew the girls made it for us, and I knew they thought Alec was going to get some based on the revealing underwear that was laid across the bed.

I pushed it aside to the floor and climbed up onto the bed where I flipped onto my back and stared up at the white ceiling. I could hear the music from downstairs and it was picking away at my already shot temper. I lifted my hand to my face and covered my eyes, coating them in darkness to try and ease the pain in my head.

I relaxed a little bit, but seconds later I jolted as a *bang* sound went off during the music, followed by two more bangs. An image from my nightmare flashed across my mind, and I screamed.

You don't deserve him.

I cried out at my own voice repeating those dreaded words to me in my head. I jumped up off my bed and ran to the corner of my room. I slid down against the wall until my behind touched the ground. I drew my knees up to my chest and placed my forehead on my knees and covered my head with my hands.

"Stop," I cried. "Please. Stop."

My nightmare was playing over and over in my mind, and it made me feel sick with fear. I heard another bang and I screamed again, but this one was different, it sounded like something hitting a hard surface.

"Keela?" Alec's shout floated into my mind.

"No!" I cried out knowing what was coming.

I was going to see him die.

I screamed when I felt hands touch me. "Stop. *Please*. Leave me alone. Get out of me head!"

The hands tightened on my arms. "Kitten, I'm here."

"Alec, just hold her." Bronagh's familiar voice filled my ears. "It's the nightmare, she is relivin' it in her conscious state."

"Nightmare?" Alec repeated. "What nightmare?"

I heard a whimper. "She's been havin' them since last year... whatever she went through... it's hauntin' her."

Aideen.

"I'm fine," I whispered.

I didn't want to upset anybody and hearing them talk even though they were talking about me, focused my mind on my reality. What I thought was happening really wasn't. It wasn't real. It was in my mind.

That was the problem though—I didn't want it on my mind.

I wanted it gone.

"She's been having nightmares? I didn't know," Alec said, his voice broken.

"None of us did, she only told us today," Bronagh's voice said.

I blew out a breath. "I'm fine," I said louder this time.

I lifted my head and opened my eyes finding all of my family standing close to me.

"I heard a bang and me mind... it just turned on me, but I'm fine now."

Alec helped me to my feet and I flushed with embarrassment.

"Please don't tell me everyone heard me?" I asked.

"Dunno, Alec kicked them out," Bronagh said and shot a glare his way.

Alec ignored Bronagh and focused on me. "We need to talk."

Oh, God.

I nodded my head.

Alec shot a look at the others and one by one they got the hint and filed out of our room.

"Love you," Aideen said to me.

I slightly smiled. "Love you too."

She closed the door after her and left Alec and myself alone in our room.

"Nightmares, really Keela?" Alec began. "Why didn't you tell me?"

I frowned. "I didn't want to worry you. I thought I could handle them. I thought they would go away."

"But they haven't?"

I shook my head. "I have them weekly. Sometimes twice a week. They're about... Darkness."

Alec lifted his hands to his face and scrubbed them. "About what you saw?"

I nodded my head. "Yes, but also... somethin' different."

Alec looked at me and waited for me to explain.

I walked over to our bed and sat down, but Alec remained standing in front of me.

"At the start of the nightmare I wake up in a hallway with blood on the walls and lots of turns, and lots of doors. I know the hallway, but can't remember where it is durin' the nightmare. When I wake up, I realise it's the hallways from Darkness. I walked them once when I was pulled out of the room we were being kept in with Bronagh... Do you remember?"

"Yes."

I nodded my head. "Yeah, well I'm there and I can hear someone callin' out to me, beggin' me to help them. I know the voice, but can't pin it to a person." I looked down. "The voice is yours, and I learn that a shadow figure is hurtin' you and you're callin' out for me to help you, but I can't. I try... I try to run as fast as I can, but I'm never quick enough... You die in the nightmare, every time. The shadow figure shoots you in the head."

Alec kneeled before me and took my shaking hands in his.

"Your brothers appear after that, and they blame me for your death. They accuse me of lettin' you die because I didn't love you. They... attack me then I switch and end up in the centre of Darkness in front of Marco. His hands are covered in blood, and I think he is the one to cover the hallway walls in blood. You brothers hold me down and tell Marco to kill me for not savin' you. I look up and Marco is gone, the shadow figure is there, but it's not just a shadow figure anymore it's me. The terror is me, I shoot myself in the head and then I wake up."

I leaned forward and pressed my forehead to Alec's.

"I'm here, and I'm not going anywhere. Do you understand me?" Alec asked.

I nodded my head.

"Tell me you understand," he said, his voice firm.

"I understand," I whispered.

He let go of my hands and cupped my face. "We're going to get you help for this. We aren't going to brush it under the carpet. This *can* be helped."

I nodded my head. "Okay," I whispered.

Alec sighed and kissed my head. "I wish I knew you were having nightmares, I wouldn't have rushed you into moving in here so quickly."

I blinked. "Do you mean that?" I asked.

Alec furrowed his eyebrows. "That I wouldn't have rushed you?"

I nodded.

"Of course I wouldn't have."

I opened my mind then and said, "You wouldn't rush me... with anythin' else then would you?"

"No, I wouldn't," Alec said, a perplexed expression on his face.

"Okay," I said, breathing easier.

Alec focused his eyes on mine. "What's on your mind? Why are you asking these questions?"

This was it.

This was the opportunity to tell Alec my feelings.

I didn't even hesitate, I looked him in the eye and said, "I don't want to get married."

Everything stopped as I waited for Alec's reply.

My breathing.

My heartbeat.

Time.

"What... what do you mean you don't want to get married?" Alec asked me, his face a few shades paler than usual.

I shook my head. "I didn't mean *not at all*, I meant I don't want to get married right now. I want us to slow down."

Alec blinked. "You want us to slow down?"

I nodded my head.

Alec was silent for a moment then he said, "Okay."

I opened my mouth to apologise to him, but when what he said registered with my brain I froze.

"O-Okay?" I repeated.

Alec nodded. "Yeah, okay. If you want us to pull back a little that's cool, we have the rest of our lives to get married, have kids, and do a bunch of other things."

I couldn't believe what I was hearing.

"I thought you would be upset with me," I admitted.

Alec laughed. "Just because I'm ready right now to take my vows and have a handful of mini me's doesn't mean you are, and that's okay."

It was?

"So you don't hate me?" I asked, my eyes filling with tears.

Alec laughed again. "No. I love you, stupid."

I laughed and my heart warmed.

"I love you too, more than me life. I don't want this to make you feel—"

"Kitten," he cut me off. "I know you love me, you don't have to question if I know that. I *know*."

I didn't know what to say.

I was not expecting this conversation to go like this.

"I... I just can't believe you aren't angry with me."

Alec leaned in and rubbed his nose against mine. "I have you. I have your heart. I'll have everything else with you in time—there is no rush. None."

I pressed my forehead to his. "I adore your love for me, I cherish it. I cherish you."

Alec smiled. "I know, Kitten."

I closed my eyes and just felt our love surround us.

After a moment Alec asked, "How long has this been bothering you?"

I thought on it then opened my eyes and said, "Ages."

Alec shook his head. "You really need to stop overthinking things. That has to be a woman thing."

I surprisingly laughed.

Alec got up and sat on our new bed and put his arm over my shoulder. "We can go back to the apartment if you want. I realise now that everything I have been doing was overwhelming you, and I want to make it right."

God, he was perfect.

I leaned into him and said, "If you asked me that this mornin' I would have jumped at the chance, but now? Not so much. I'm so relieved after our talk, and being here with you doesn't scare me anymore... it excites me."

Alec squeezed me. "Are you sure?"

I nodded my head.

"I'm so sure I'm practically deodorant," I teased.

Alec laughed and kissed my head.

I remained next to him for a few minutes until a knock rapped on the bedroom door.

"Come in," I called out.

The door opened and Nico's head popped around the door. "Everything okay?" he asked.

Alec and I nodded.

"Great." He smiled, then dropped it. "Alec, we need you to come and help us with something."

I wondered what 'something' was, and so did Alec.

"Can't you just—"

"Alec," Nico cut him off, and gave him a stern look.

The look was code for something.

"Sure. I'll help," Alec said then turned to me. "You're okay, right?"

I nodded my head.

After getting everything off my chest and clearing the air I was *so* okay.

Alec left our room with Nico, and I went in search of the girls. I called out to them, and found them in the sitting room, with glasses in their hands. Bronagh was in the middle of cracking open a bottle of wine.

"Don't drink until we're back!" Nico's voice shouted then the front door slammed shut.

Bronagh ignored him and poured wine into the glasses extended to her.

"Where are they goin'?" I asked the girls.

They all shrugged. "No clue," Branna said. "You doin' okay?"

I nodded my head. "Much better."

Bronagh howled, "Park your arse and grab a glass, we're havin' a housewarmin' party even if it's just the four of us."

"You mean *five* of us," a voice from behind us said.

I jumped and turned around. "Alannah," I breathed. "You frightened me."

Alannah Ryan, Bronagh's best friend, and my friend, grinned. "Nico let me in as he and the brothers were goin' out."

Bronagh whooped and poured Alannah a glass of wine.

I looked between the girls and shook my head.

This wasn't going to end well.

Chapter Eleven

The girls were hiding from me.

I couldn't find the bitches anywhere.

I was resorting to looking in every room of my house to fucking find them. I was about to pass by mine and Alec's bedroom when I heard giggling. I opened the door and followed the giggling to the bathroom.

"What are you four doin' in here?" I asked as I entered the gigantic bathroom of my master bedroom.

Four heads quickly looked in my direction, three of the gazes were hazy and clouded with alcohol and one was clear and teasing. Alannah raised her hands in front of her chest and chuckled. "Don't look at me, this was *their* idea."

Uh-oh.

Branna, Aideen, and Bronagh having ideas when sober usually ended in disaster, drunken ideas would surely be worse.

"*What* was their idea?" I asked and placed my hands on my hips.

I stared the three eejits down hoping to be somewhat intimidating, but when they burst into a fit of giggles I knew my threatening glare was little more than a slap on the wrist to them.

I switched my gaze to Alannah and softened it. "What did they do?"

"Somethin' stupid," Alannah chuckled and shook her head.

Bronagh shoved her. "You took one too, so shut it."

Alannah balked at her. "You forced me. You literally pulled my trousers and knickers down!"

That statement sent the three musketeers into another fit of laughter.

"Have you ever heard of waxin'?" Aideen asked, then fell into the bathtub as she burst into uncontrollable laughter. Bronagh and Branna were wheezing from laughing so hard.

I wanted to laugh simply because they were laughing, but I had to keep my no-bullshit expression on my face to get to the bottom of what the hell they did.

Alannah angrily folded her arms across her chest and glared at Aideen. "It's *winter* time, who gets a wax during this season? Give me a break!"

I looked between all the faces before me and felt the beginnings of a headache form in the base of my skull.

"What the hell went on in here?" I asked. "You forced Alannah to get semi naked with you all, to what? Jump her bones?"

Bronagh put her hand in the air like she was a student in primary school, and I was the teacher waiting to give her permission to speak.

I couldn't help but grin as I said, "Yeah, Bee, what is it?"

"Can you tell Dominic what you think happened? He will be so hot for me, thinkin' that I was strippin' Lana that he will overlook me drinkin' this early."

I snorted. "Don't use me to soften up your lad, they *all* told you wait until they got back before crackin' open the wine. You three can deal with those impendin' arguments on your own."

Aideen put her up hand next and that move did make me laugh

because she was in fact the educator out of the five of us.

"What is it, Ado?" I asked.

"I'm not in a relationship with any of the brothers so they can't say shite to me," she said proudly from her spot in the bathtub.

Branna rolled her eyes. "Please, you and Kane argue most out of the lot of us. You two are practically in a relationship, but don't kiss, have sex, or do anythin' intimate... you're in an enemyship."

Aideen seethed in silence while we all chuckled at Branna's very correct observation.

Alannah grunted to me, "Can you get back to you givin' out to them for forcing me to—"

"We didn't force you, you wanted to do it for fun too. I could see it in your freckled face!" Bronagh cut Alannah off and laughed with her sister.

I raised my hands to my temples and rubbed. "What the hell did the four of you do?"

Things were eerily silent for a moment until Aideen cracked it with a giggle. "We took pregnancy tests."

I blinked my eyes and stared at her.

"You took pregnancy tests?" I repeated.

"Yes," Bronagh giggled. "Just for fun."

I continued to blink and stare as I silently judged my group of friends.

They were such morons.

"Okay, so you took pregnancy tests... you better have thrown them in the bin and washed the counter down—if I find piss anywhere in here I'm stickin' your noses in it," I warned.

Bronagh gasped. "Like a dog?"

"Exactly." I grinned. "Just like a dog."

Bronagh widened her eyes and it made Branna laugh. "Would you relax? We cleaned up and we'll wipe down the counter again when we're done with the tests."

That piqued my interest.

"You mean you aren't already done with them?" I asked.

Branna shook her head. "We're waitin' for—"

Someone's phone let out a shrill sound cutting Branna off and causing her, and the other girls to grin.

"We were waitin' for *that* alarm," she finished.

I rolled my eyes. "Well, go on then. Look and then throw them in the bin."

All four of the girls remained still.

"Oh, shite. I can't do it," Bronagh said as her complexion suddenly paled.

"I can't either," the other three morons mumbled in unison.

I threw my hands up in the air. "Why did you take them if you're too afraid to see the results?"

Bronagh wiped her brow with the back of her hand. "Because it dawned on me that I could be pregnant. Me and Dominic have been tryin' for months."

I stared at her. "So why can't you look?"

"Because it's terrifyin'!" she replied.

"Oh, for the love of God," I grumbled and pushed them out of the way. "I'll bloody do it."

I stumbled forward, but when Alannah didn't move aside right away it caused me to fall into the counter. I caught myself and wasn't hurt, but my forearm sent the pregnancy tests into the sink.

"Shite," I said and quickly gathered them.

I wasn't worried about them being tampered, they all had the caps on the end where you urinate. I just had no clue which stick was whose because they were all the same brand of pregnancy test.

"Now we don't know which test is which!" Aideen groaned and got out of my bathtub.

Alannah snorted. "One will definitely be negative, I can't remember the last time I had sex."

Bronagh grinned. "I do, it was six months ago and you said your one night stand was *way* better than... What's the insult you dubbed him with? Was it Snowflake?"

"Bronagh!" Alannah gasped. "We're not discussin' *him*!"

Him?

"Who is *him*? Who is Snowflake?" I asked.

Alannah glared at Bronagh. "Don't," she warned.

Bronagh ignored Alannah and looked to me as she said, "Damien."

I remained quiet for a second then said, "Damien Slater?"

Bronagh nodded her head then hissed when Alannah thumped her in the arm.

Branna and Aideen giggled as Bronagh grumbled and rubbed her arm.

"You had a *thing* with Damien?" I asked Alannah.

She groaned. "It was one night *years* ago, it is *not* a big deal. Seriously. We were kids."

Bronagh gave Alannah a knowing look. "You're lyin' through your teeth and you know it."

Alannah sighed, but remained silent.

I was shocked.

"You *shagged* Damien?" I asked.

Things were silent for a moment then everyone burst into laughter, including Alannah.

"Dude, nice one. Damien is fit!" Aideen said then high-fived Alannah who was shaking her head.

"Hey!" Bronagh frowned.

Aideen rolled her eyes. "I said Damien, not Dominic."

Bronagh deadpanned, "They're identical twins."

"Can't be, they have different hair colour," Aideen said, waving Bronagh off.

Bronagh shook her head. "I said that too, but they both informed me it didn't mean anythin'. Even with the different hair colour they have matching DNA—they're identical twins. It's very rare for twins to have different eye colour or hair colour because their DNA is a blueprint match, but Dominic and Damien are that very small percentile of identical twins with different hair colour. Argue against it all you want, but that's how it is."

KEELA

Aideen was silent for a moment. "Okay... but I still think Damien is hotter. Sorry, not sorry."

I laughed. "You never met him—neither of us have. How can you think he is hotter than Dominic? That lad is ripped."

"Girls, that's me fella you're both—"

"Because I'm around Dominic so much that I think of him as a kid brother. He *is* the same age as Gavin after all."

I pinched the bridged of my nose. "Damien is the same age too... We *just* discussed them being *identical twins* meaning they're possibly minutes apart in age."

Aideen snorted. "Yeah, but Damien could be a boy toy that I could—"

"I *beg* you not to finish that sentence!" Branna suddenly cut Aideen off and heaved.

I laughed and looked at Aideen. "I'm tellin' Kane you want to shag his little brother."

"I'm gonna be sick," Bronagh mumbled.

Aideen grinned. "Make sure I'm present when you do."

"You're twisted," I stated, but smirked.

"You speak the truth," Aideen replied, not fazed by my insult.

Alannah held her hands up in the air. "Can we get *off* the Damien topic, please?"

"You mean the Snowflake topic?"

Bronagh cracked up laughing. "I *love* that insult, so much better than Fuckface."

I chuckled and looked at Alannah.

She didn't look angry.

She looked sad.

I momentarily wondered what that was about.

"Sure, we can get of the topic," I murmured then looked down to my hands.

I flicked through the pregnancy tests. "Negative, negative, negative, nega—Wait, what?"

"What?" the four girls shouted in unison.

I stared down at the pregnancy test in my right hand with wide eyes. "This one is positive."

All of the girls gasped.

"Fuck off!" Aideen snapped.

"You're messin!" Bronagh accused.

"I'll cry if you're playin'," Branna whispered.

"It's not mine," Alannah stated.

I looked up from the positive pregnancy test then lifted it in the air and flipped it around so each girl could clearly see the visible pink plus sign.

"I'm dead serious, it's positive."

"Omigod!" the girls cried.

I was shaking.

One of the girls was pregnant... but which one?

"Why didn't you mark the bloody tests so you knew which one was whose?" I snapped.

"Because we weren't expectin' you, aka he-woman, to crash into the counter and knock them all into the bloody sink!" Aideen bellowed back.

I felt like I was about to throw up.

"So one of you is pregnant, but we don't know who?" I asked.

Bronagh had tears in her eyes. "Dominic and me are tryin' and Ryder and Branna don't use protection and she came off birth control last month so it could be either of us. Alannah had sex six months ago so it's not her... Aideen, what about you?"

Aideen was pale. "Could be. I had unprotected sex a good few weeks ago with a one night stand."

Oh, for Christ sakes.

"Fuckin' hell, Aideen," I growled.

"I know," she snapped. "I know it was stupid, you don't need to convince me of what I already know."

I rubbed my pounding head. "Take more tests to see which one of you it is."

Bronagh nodded her head and quickly jumped up and opened

my medicine cabinet. She pushed aside a few things and then gasped. "There are none left."

Bloody hell.

"We'll have to go get more," I said and placed my hands on my hips.

"If I move I'm gonna puke everywhere," Bronagh informed me.

"Me too," Branna mumbled.

I glanced to Aideen who looked like she was about to fall over and I groaned.

"Look after them," I said to Alannah. "I'll go get the stupid tests."

Alannah nodded her head to me as I walked out of my bathroom and descended the stairs.

This was all I needed.

I had enough on my mind without worrying about the girls.

I was so consumed with my thoughts as I stepped off the bottom step of my staircase that I forgot about my surroundings and walked head first into a chest. I stumbled backward, but arms gripped onto my shoulders and held me steady.

"Whoa, careful, sweetheart."

I stood motionless as I opened my eyes and stared at my unexpected houseguest.

"What are *you* doin' here?" I asked, my voice a growl.

"Now, now. That's no way to talk to your uncle."

CHAPTER TWELVE

"Cut the bullshit, Uncle Brandon," I said and stepped back away from him. "What are you doin' here? How the hell did you get in here?"

My uncle dropped his arms to his sides and frowned at me. "I'm here for your housewarmin' party."

The stupid, fucking housewarming party.

How the hell did he even know about it?

I was going to *kill* Alec for arranging it.

"Now is a bad time, I've stuff to do and—"

"Keela," my uncle cut me off. "Calm down and take a breath."

I did as he said and took a nice deep breath.

"Good." My uncle nodded.

My pounding head worsened by the second, and the sight of my uncle didn't help matters.

"Why are you here? I thought we agreed to havin' lunch once a month. *Once.*"

He was lucky I agreed to seeing him once a month, I found it hard to be around him now. Especially with my nightmares, I was worried about what I would see.

My uncle snorted. "I wanted to see you, so sue me."

I grunted, "I can't be dealin' with this right now."

"Is everythin' okay?" my uncle asked.

I sighed. "Yes, everythin' is fine, but the party is not happenin' anymore so you will have to—"

"What do you mean the party isn't happenin' anymore? We drove over here for *nothin'*?"

I recognised that voice, and I glared at my uncle. "You didn't."

Uncle Brandon groaned, "You and your *cousin* haven't spoken in over a *year*."

"She bailed on me weddin'!" Micah's shrill tone shouted, filling my ears.

Jesus... why are you doing this to me?

I wanted to cry. "I *had* to leave, Micah... and we haven't spoken because you won't give me the time of day."

Micah scoffed and stepped out from behind her father. "Why *did* you leave?"

I looked to my uncle and he gave me a gentle shake of his head indicating he didn't tell her why.

I looked backed to Micah and said, "Because Storm was hit by a van and almost died. I needed to be here to sign his vet form or they couldn't perform the operation he needed to survive."

My uncle raised his eyebrows with surprise.

I couldn't blame him—I was shocked I told the semi-lie so easily.

Storm *did* almost die, but that happened because of different circumstances days after I arrived back in Ireland from Micah's wedding in the Bahamas. The reason I came home was because of Alec... and my uncle... and two other vile creatures that I refused to think about.

"It was me *weddin'* though, Keela." Micah frowned.

I refrained from rolling my eyes. "And Storm is me dog, I wasn't lettin' him die. I was there for the most part of the trip though, isn't that somethin'? I still went."

Micah thought on that before sighing, "Yeah, I guess."

Fuck.

She agreed with me.

I opened my mouth to speak just as the hall door open and in walked Alec and his brothers.

He groaned when he spotted my uncle. "I'm going to kill Gavin," he said.

Gavin Collins?

"Why?" I asked.

"He told *them* about the party when Aideen rang and told him. We tried to get them to leave before you and the girls came down the stairs. That's why Dominic called Alec down from your room, we wanted his help." Kane replied, glaring at my uncle.

He really didn't like him.

Wait, how the hell did Gavin tell my uncle about the party— "Keela, come here?" Alec said to me, breaking my train of thought.

I walked over to Alec just as music started up again from the sitting room. Everyone went inside and left us out in the hallway. Seconds passed and then I heard laughter.

So much for the damn party being over!

"I'll go and get rid of them."

"Leave them," I sighed and turned to Alec. "They're fine. Will you just go up to our bathroom and tell the girls to come down?"

Alec nodded his head and jogged up the stairs.

I went down to my kitchen to get some water and was surprised when I found Gavin leaning against my back door having a cigarette.

"Hey," I said to him.

He flicked his smoke away. "Hey, nice house."

I snorted. "Thanks."

Gavin closed the back door and turned to me.

He looked so... different.

Black jeans, boots, buttoned up blue shirt, and a snapback hat on his head.

KEELA

He looked... hot.

"When did you get here?" I asked. "And how did you get in?"

Gavin grinned. "Front door was open, I came with..."

"You came with *who*?" I asked.

Gavin avoided looking me in the eye. "Your uncle."

My uncle?

"Why would you come with—Wait, why are you around me uncle in the first place?"

Gavin scratched the back of his elbow. "Well... he is me boss."

Excuse me?

"That's not funny," I said.

Gavin shrugged his shoulders. "I'm not laughin'."

My stomach churned. "You can't be serious... You can't get involved with me uncle's... business."

Gavin snorted.

"Gavin, I'm serious!" I snapped. "Do *not* get involved with me uncle."

Gavin gnawed on his lower lip. "Too late, Kay."

What the hell?

"What do you mean 'Too late'?" I asked.

Gavin groaned, "I can't really talk about this—"

"Brandon!" I bellowed, cutting Gavin off and stormed out of my kitchen.

My uncle walked out of the sitting room with raised hands. "Whatever it is, I can fix it."

I jammed my thumb over my shoulder. "You... *enlisted* me best friend's *little brother*? Really?"

Brandon sighed. "The kid won't be doing anythin' dangerous, just a couple of runs here and there till he finds his feet among me circle."

His 'circle' was his group of baby gangsters, how lads and girls started out in his world.

No!

"I don't want him to find his feet. How dare you do this!" I yelled.

My uncle pinched the bridge of his nose. "He came to me, not the other way around. If you want to be annoyed, be annoyed at the kid."

I swung around and narrowed my eyes at Gavin who was leaning against the kitchen doorway. "I'm twenty-two, Keela. That's the same age as Dominic, Damien, and Bronagh. I'm not a kid."

I felt sick—he had no idea what getting involved with my uncle meant.

"I'm tellin' your brothers," I warned.

Gavin snorted, "So?"

He wasn't afraid?

His older brothers were big, and scary as hell when mad.

"Fine... I'll tell Aideen," I snarled.

Gavin stood upright. "Don't you dare."

Ha! I had him now.

"I am! I'm tellin' her!" I turned around and walked by my chuckling uncle.

I was about to call for Aideen when she walked down the stairs with Bronagh, Branna, and Alannah behind her.

Perfect timing.

"I need to talk to you!" I said to Aideen.

Bronagh leaned forward. "When are you goin' to the shops?" she whispered.

"Soon. I promise."

Bronagh nodded her head as I grabbed Aideen's arm and lead her down the hallway.

"What's wrong?" she asked.

Gavin came up behind her. "Nothin', Keela is just stickin' her nose in places she shouldn't."

The neck of the little bastard!

"I'm tryin' to stop you from makin' a mistake you little shite!"

Aideen turned and stared between her brother and me. "Talk. Now."

Uh-oh.

Mama bear Aideen was rearing her head.

Her mother died giving birth to Gavin, and as the only daughter in the midst of four brothers and a father, she moulded into a mother figure in the household even though she was the second youngest. She took care of Gavin the most out of everyone in her family. He was the baby of the family and Aideen adored him.

"Go ahead, Gav," I said. "Tell her about your new... *job*."

Gavin growled at me, "You're such a fuckin' bitch."

"Hey!" Aideen snapped and whacked him across the head. "Don't you speak to her like that."

She turned to me then and said, "Tell me what's happenin'."

"Gavin has entered me uncle's circle. He works for him now."

Aideen stared at me for a long moment then turned to Gavin and began to slap the shite out of him.

"Damn it, Aideen!" Gavin shouted and tried to dodge away from her hands. "Stop!"

Aideen was shouting obscenities.

"You stupid little eejit! How could you? Do you understand what you have gotten yourself into?" she asked, her voice high.

Gavin grabbed her hands and stared down at her. "Yes, I do. I can handle this."

"Brandon is a *gangster*!" Aideen cried, but kept her voice low.

Gavin sighed. "I'm aware of that, but he is also an honourable man."

I snorted. "And how the hell would you know that?"

Gavin cut his eyes to me. "Because I hang around with Jason and have gotten to know him."

A gasp came from behind Gavin so he looked over his shoulder and groaned. "Bronagh... let me explain."

"You pal around with Jason? As in *Jason Bane!*" Bronagh asked, her eyes wide.

Gavin hung his head. "Yeah, he's a mate now."

Bronagh lost her head.

"How can you be friends with Jason Bane? He was horrible to me in school, you *know* that!" she shouted.

"He fucked me over, you know *that* as well!" I growled reminding Gavin that Jason Bane was not favoured by us girls.

He was a wank stain.

"I'm beginnin' to feel like I'm not welcome here."

No. Fucking. Way.

We all turned our attention to the doorway of my sitting room and gaped.

"Nice to see everyone, too," the bastard himself smirked.

I didn't understand how or why he was here.

"You... get out. Right now!" I snapped.

Jason held his hands up in front of his chest. "Fine. I don't need to be told twice. I'll get me coat."

He turned and walked into my sitting room as Brandon and Micah exited the room. Ryder, Nico, and Kane walked out of the kitchen and joined the rest of us in the hallway.

"I'm guessin' the party is over." My uncle grinned.

I rolled my eyes. "Just leave. I'll talk to you later."

My uncle chuckled, then walked over and kissed my forehead, before he nodded to everyone else and walked out of my house. Micah didn't look at me as she followed. Gavin walked out behind them and Aideen ran out after him shouting and demanding he listen to her.

I groaned, "Go, make sure she doesn't kill him."

Bronagh, Branna and Alannah were already out the door, and the brothers were right behind them. I shook my head and went into my sitting room where I found Jason sitting on my sofa.

I saw red.

"Get. Out," I snarled.

He stood and sighed. "We can't talk then?"

Talk?

"About bloody what?" I asked.

Jason shrugged. "You look good."

I narrowed my eyes. "Don't you dare."

"I can't say you look good?" Jason grinned.

"I don't know what game you're playin', but knock it off and leave."

I was surprised when Jason closed the space between us and slid his hands around my waist. My reflexes weren't quick enough—scratch that they were worth shite because I froze as Jason kissed me.

He. Kissed. Me.

This bastard destroyed me three years ago, he was married to my cousin and now... now he fucking kissed me?

I saw no logic in that.

None.

I yanked my head back from Jason and screamed.

I don't know if I screamed words, or just made noise.

I tried to push away from him, but he was pulled from me with a force that caused me to stumble. I regained my footing and looked to Jason... who was being pulled away from me by a furious looking Alec.

Fuck.

CHAPTER THIRTEEN

"Alec!" I screamed and jumped backwards when he speared Jason to the ground.

I reached for Alec's shoulder in the hope I could pull him off Jason, but there was too much movement and I was not risking getting hurt to save Jason from a few punches that he bloody well deserved. I stood back and continued to shout at the pair to stop. I screamed for Bronagh when I spotted her at the sitting room doorway.

"Get Dominic!" I yelled.

She frantically nodded her head then turned and ran out of the house.

I looked back to Alec and Jason, and noticed Jason was now somehow on top of Alec and throwing punches at his face. I wasn't sure if one of them broke through Alec's guard or not, but I wasn't risking it. I jumped on Jason's back and wrapped my arms around his neck.

"Stop it!" I shouted into his ear.

Jason violently pushed his body back and I fell off him and onto the floor with a thud.

"Keela!" Alec screamed then turned his attention back to Jason. "You motherfucker!"

I groaned on the floor as I held onto my throbbing shoulder. I took in a few breaths and sat upright. I stumbled as I got to my feet, and rolled my shoulder to make sure it wasn't seriously injured. It hurt, but it moved so I knew the worst that would come from my fall would be a bruise.

I looked back down to Jason and Alec. Alec was back on top, and I felt like they were just about to break apart. I was preparing myself to jump in-between them, but when Gavin appeared at the doorway of my sitting room and narrowed his eyes at Alec and Jason, I gasped. Gavin shot into the room and kicked Alec in the side at full force. Alec hunched forward a little, but he jabbed his right hand out and caught Gavin in the stomach causing him to double over in pain.

"That's what you get!" I bellowed and rushed at him.

I shoved him in the chest and knocked him onto his back on the floor. He groaned and held onto his stomach and dry heaved.

"Don't you dare get sick on the new floor you prick!" I screamed.

"Keela?" Nico's roar sounded from outside my house.

I shoved Gavin back down when he tried to get up.

"Sittin' room!" I shouted.

I turned back to Jason and Alec when a glass shattering sound rang throughout the room.

I gasped.

My glass vase was shattered into hundreds of pieces on the floor, and the flowers Mr. Pervert got me were tangled in the glass shards.

"You bastard!" I shouted at Jason who was pushing himself up off the floor. Alec was also trying to get up, but the water on the floor from the broken vase caused him to slip. Jason got to his feet and angled his body at Alec. He reached for the clock that was sitting on top of my fireplace and raised it above his head.

He was going to hit Alec in the head with it.

I screamed in horror.

I felt a rush of wind brush by my body then all of a sudden Nico was there, standing between Jason and Alec. Nico knocked the clock out of Jason's hands and punched him directly across the jaw knocking Jason on his arse. The relief I felt when Jason was disarmed hit me full force, and I burst into tears. I quickly moved to Alec and helped him to his feet. He was wet from the vase water, but also groaning in pain and it worried me.

"Are you okay?" he asked as fat tears rolled down my cheeks.

Me?

He was the one bleeding!

"I'm fine!" I cried. "Are you?"

Alec growled, "Let me kill him and I'll be fine."

"What the fuck happened?" Nico shouted as he shoved Jason to the floor.

"That fucker kissed Keela!" Alec snapped.

Nico growled and turned and kicked Jason in the stomach.

"That's for kissin' my bro's girl, and this," he kicked him again, "is because I hate your sorry ass."

I looked to Gavin when he groaned and I saw red. "How could you!" I screamed. "How could you side with Jason over us? You *attacked* Alec, Gavin. You attacked me fiancé! I am done with you do you understand me? Done!"

Gavin stumbled to his feet. "Kay... he is the son-in-law of me boss, and he's me mate. I had to help him."

That wasn't good enough.

"Your boss is *my* uncle, I rank higher than Jason ever will!" I snapped.

I wanted to shove Gavin out of my house so I marched over and grabbed him by the ear and pulled at him. "Get out. Now!"

Gavin wriggled to get free but couldn't without having his ear ripped off. He opened his mouth to speak, but a loud growl cut him off. We all looked to the sitting room doorway where Storm was stood. His stance was one of preparing for an attack, and he had his teeth bared indicating what he was about to do.

I jumped away from Gavin as Storm ran for him. Gavin cursed and jumped over my sofa and stumbled out of the sitting room. Strom slipped on the wooden floor in the hallway, but continued to give chase to Gavin. I knew Gavin got out of the house before Storm could get to him, when the front door slammed shut.

I looked to Storm when he came back into the sitting room. I didn't go over to him, I waited until he came to me. I knew he wasn't dangerous and I knew he wouldn't hurt me, but I didn't want to do anything to upset him when he was clearly stressed.

I kneeled down and rubbed and hugged him when he put his head against my leg. I kissed his head and scratched his ears. "Thank you," I murmured to him for protecting me.

"Good boy, Storm," Alec's voice praised. "Protecting Mama."

I turned my head when Jason's voice snarled, "Don't even think of settin' that beast on me."

I glared at him. "It's no more than you deserve!" I snapped. "What the hell did you think you were playin' at, showin' up at me house and kissin' me? Have you lost your mind?"

Jason smirked, blood smeared over his nose and mouth. "Nope, I just enjoy a bit of excitement every now and then."

Nico reached down and punched Jason across the face.

"Is that exciting enough for you?" he asked.

I shook my head and got to my feet. I brought Storm to my kitchen and put him inside and closed the door. When I walked back to the sitting room I stood idle at the doorway and watched as Nico pushed Jason out of the room. Neither of them looked at me.

I put my arm around Alec who walked out of the sitting room holding onto his side. I growled and I pressed myself to him. "I'll kill Gavin for hurtin' you."

Alec shook his head. "Aideen will do a great job of doing that herself."

I didn't smile because I knew she would. She would beat the crap out of him for betraying us like he did. I leaned up to kiss Alec, but I froze when I heard a siren. A Garda car siren.

"Fuck!" Alec grunted.

We walked outside and I groaned when I spotted two male Garda getting out of their squad car and walking into our garden. I wanted to cry because I had no clue what we were going to do.

"Can I help you officers?" my uncle's voice sounded.

I looked to my right and raised my eyebrows as my uncle walked over to the Garda like he wasn't repulsed. I knew better though. My uncle hated the law and anyone who represented it.

"We received a noise complaint... and from the looks of the blood on some of you I'm guessin' some fall outs happened?" one of Garda mused as Gavin and Jason leaned against my uncle's SUV.

Micah was inside the SUV on her phone, she didn't even care about the bullshit her stupid husband had just caused.

"Fuckin' bitch," I growled.

I refocused on my uncle and the Garda and walked forward with Alec when we were motioned to do so.

"This is my niece and her fiancé's house. Anythin' that happened here was... resolved. I assure you."

Both Garda raised their eyebrows at my uncle. "What is your name, sir?" one asked.

"Brandon Daley."

I watched as both of the Garda exchanged a look.

"Mr. Daley... would you like to speak to us over by the car, Sir?"

"Absolutely," my uncle replied.

I shook my head in disgust as the trio walked away from Alec and myself.

"They're about to end up on his payroll," I grumbled. "I hate crooked Garda."

Alec gave me a squeeze. "I'll square this with Brandy. I won't be in debt to him for helping us."

I scoffed. "He wouldn't dare hold you in his debt, I'll have his balls if he even tried."

I glanced to Ryder and Kane as they brought Branna, Alannah and a distraught Aideen, back inside my house. Nico and Bronagh remained outside with us. My uncle re-joined us when his 'talk' with the Garda ended and they drove off in their car.

"You're unbelievable," I said to him.

He simply shrugged then switched his gaze to Alec. "That's me son-in-law you and your brother just roughed up."

I opened my mouth to speak, but Alec bet me to it. "That's my fiancée your son-in-law just kissed."

My uncle growled and looked over to Jason who raised his hands in the air. "I was just playin'!"

Bullshit.

"I'll deal with you later," my uncle snarled then turned back to me, and softened his gaze.

"I'm sorry about all this."

I nodded my head to him.

My uncle looked to Nico then. "Son… can I have a word?"

I stepped forward. "What do you want with him?" I asked.

Nico appeared next to me. "It's okay, Kay. I'll deal with this."

My uncle smirked and moved off to the end of my garden with Nico. A few words were shared then Nico shook my uncle's hand.

"Dominic!" Bronagh and I snapped in unison.

I think Bronagh knew just as well as me that some sort of deal was struck between the pair, and that wasn't good. Not at all.

"I'll talk to you later, honey." My uncle winked at me then walked over to his Jeep.

I ignored him and focused on Gavin. "You come back here again and I'll kill you meself, do you understand me?"

Gavin didn't know what to say, I could tell by the look on his face, so he turned and got into the back of my uncle's SUV. My uncle laughed. "You're definitely me niece."

"Lucky me," I sarcastically hissed.

My uncle got into his SUV chuckling, Jason got in grunting and groaning in pain, which made me grin. Fuck that bastard. I turned my attention from the SUV when it reversed out of my garden and looked to Nico as he walked towards us, his gaze locked on Bronagh.

"What the hell was that?" she snapped.

Nico swallowed. "He offered me a job."

Alec shot forward and shoved Nico.

"Wait!" Nico shouted. "It's a good one, it's for fighting."

Alec halted his beating on his brother and stared at him. "He's paying you to fight?"

Nico nodded. "Every week at Darkness for a fixed wage... I need this Alec, fitness training isn't enough to pay my bills. I need to take care of my girl."

Alec let go of Nico and shook his head, but I could already see he accepted Nico's job, but Bronagh... she didn't.

"I'm goin' home, and you're *not* to follow me," she said, her voice tight with emotion.

She walked out of my garden and left us looking after her.

"You aren't going after her?" Alec murmured.

Nico shook his head. "I will only upset her more if I do. She needs to cool off. When she is calm I'll explain why this is no different than the arranged fights I take part in every so often."

I humourlessly laughed. "You're so fuckin' stupid, you don't see what she does."

Nico looked at me. "Which is what?"

"Me uncle, in her eyes, is Marco. You've gone back to a world she hates... and you made Darkness part of the deal... do you even realise what that place does to her? What it does to me?"

Nico didn't speak. He didn't do anything.

I turned from him and Alec and walked into my house, not looking back when both of them called for me.

Chapter Fourteen

"I'm goin' to *kill* Gavin," Aideen said for the tenth time in the last twenty minutes.

I sighed. "I'll help you."

My attempt at humour was lost on her.

"I can't believe he would do this. I can't believe he would join your uncle's circle. Me brothers will kill him!" she swore.

I sat in silence but then looked to Branna when she called my name. She was sat to my right on my sofa with Alannah, Kane, Alec, and Nico spread out on it too. All of them were looking over at Aideen and myself.

"Yeah?" I replied.

She gave me a stern look. "You have to go to the shops... remember?"

I was about to ask for what, but widened my eyes when I remembered.

The pregnancy tests.

"Fuck," I murmured. "I'll go now."

Branna nodded, but didn't look at the brothers when they looked at her.

"Go to the shop for what?" Aideen asked me.

I looked at her. "You *know* for what."

She shook her head.

Oh, for God's sakes.

"The bathroom," I said, staring at her as I drilled the answer into her mind with my eyes.

She gasped when it hit her.

"The pregnancy tests!" she shouted.

I face-palmed myself.

"Pregnancy tests?" male voices shouted in unison.

"Well done," I growled to Aideen who had her hand over her mouth.

I looked to the brothers who were all on their feet. "Yeah, pregnancy tests."

"Who is pregnant?" Alec asked and stared at me.

I shook my head. "Not me."

He visibly relaxed. "Thank God. I mean, I want babies with you, but we just talked about—"

"It's okay, I know." I snorted and shook my head again.

"If not you, then who?" Ryder asked.

I looked to Branna and he almost fell over.

"Bran?" he asked.

She winced. "It might be me. *Might* be."

Ryder looked like he was about to puke.

Kane scratched his head. "I don't understand what's going on. So Branna might be pregnant?"

Aideen nodded her head. "Or Bronagh."

"What?" Nico screamed.

I jumped with fright at the pitch of it.

"Why are you screamin'? You and Bronagh are tryin' for a baby."

Nico fell back onto the sofa. "We are but… still. Fuck."

"Relax honey," Branna said to Nico. "It might not be Bronagh either."

"Who else could it be then?" Alec asked.

Both Branna and I looked at Aideen.

She hissed. "Thanks very much!"

I shrugged my shoulders. "Should have kept your big mouth shut."

"Aideen?" Kane's voice snapped. "You might be pregnant? By fucking who?"

That was a good question.

Aideen lifted her hand to her head. "We're not doin' this. We aren't agruin' when we have no idea who is pregnant."

"Then let's fucking find out," Kane growled.

I blinked at him.

He was furious.

I spoke softly. "I'll go get some in Tesco—"

"I'll go with you," Kane cut me off then stormed out of the sitting room, and then out of the house.

"Fuck," Aideen hissed.

She stormed off up the stairs, and Branna and Alannah quickly followed her. I sighed and looked back to the remaining brothers. "I'll be back."

Ryder and Nico nodded at me, but they were both in a world of their own.

I moved over to Alec and leaned up to kiss him.

"I love you," he whispered.

I smiled. "Why are you whisperin'?" I asked.

"Because they're all in deep shit with their ladies, and I'm cool with you. I don't want to pour salt in their wounds by shoving it in their faces."

"Then learn to whisper, you prick," Nico growled making me smile.

I kissed Alec again.

"I love you, Kitten," he repeated. "I really do."

I relished in hearing that.

"And I love you, Playboy. To Neptune and back."

"Good, now go and get those pregnancy tests before me and my brothers lose our minds. I want to know if it's one of the sisters. I hope so, I want to be an Uncle," Alec said, chuckling.

Ryder and Nico dove for Alec as I ran out of the house giggling to myself. I stopped smiling and making sounds when I climbed into Alec's SUV and looked to Kane in the driver's seat.

"You okay?" I asked.

He nodded. "Fine."

He took off driving then and I took his hint of wanting silence loud and clear. We got to Tesco a few minutes later and exited the car. We walked side by side into the shop and Kane trailed me as I headed for the hygiene aisle.

"Fuck me," Kane whistled. "That's a lot of different brands."

I nodded my head. "Yep. There is a lot to choose from."

Kane lifted his hand to his head. "Can't we just pick any box? I want to get out of here."

I snickered.

"Feelin' uncomfortable being in the women's aisle?" I teased.

He shook his head then stumbled a little to the side.

"I just... I just want to leave," he said, his voice low.

I dropped my smile and stepped toward him. "Kane... are you okay?" I asked.

"I don't... I don't know. I don't feel good," he said.

The next few seconds passed by in slow motion. Kane turned to face me, but he lost his footing. He grabbed at thin air as he fell to the ground looking for something to stop his fall, but found nothing. I heard myself scream when his body hit the floor and his eyes closed and didn't re-open.

"KANE!" I cried and dropped to my knees next to him.

I placed my hands on his face and shook him. "Wake up!" I screamed.

Nothing.

He was breathing, I could tell that from his chest movements, but he was unconscious and not responding to me. That frightened the life out of me. I shook him a few times and shouted his name hoping to get his attention, but he didn't wake up. He didn't move, or flinch.

He just laid there.

He gets ill now and then, but he has never collapsed... he hasn't even mentioned lately that he wasn't feeling good.

Something was *very* wrong.

I looked up and down the aisle and was surprised when I found nobody at either end. I could hear multiple fast paced footsteps though, and people calling all different things out to me to see which aisle I was on. I placed my hands on Kane's chest and screamed.

"Somebody help me!"

KANE

CHAPTER ONE

I had a headache.

A pounding headache.

My stomach was queasy too, and I felt a little dizzy.

I felt like shite.

I felt like this because I was scared.

I was *so* damn scared... and all because of a damn plastic stick!

I tried not to look at the stick that would decide my fate as I sat in the main bathroom of the Slater brothers' house. I focused on the tiled floor, and the grout that cemented them in place to avoid looking up. I counted the tiles, and each time I only got to ten or eleven before my head automatically turned to look at the counter.

No.

I hissed at myself and stilled my movements before I could take a peek. I didn't want to know what the stupid stick said, but I had to. It was eating away at me and has been for the last hour and a half. I looked up at the ceiling and blinked.

I wish you were here, ma.

I needed my mother, I needed to vent to somebody about the fucked up day I had. I swallowed and pictured my ma was in front of me, and I mentally unloaded everything onto her. I told her everything.

Today was a pretty eventful day to say the least.

It was moving day for Keela and Alec. They moved out of their box-sized apartment into a beautiful house, directly across from the brothers' place in Upton. As a member of the friendship group we uphold, we were all drafted in to help pack up boxes in the old apartment and then unpack them in the new house.

Everyone had some fun packing up the apartment and unpacking in the new house, but we also had arguments… and a lot of other bullshit to deal with. Keela had more bullshit than anyone to deal with.

My girl was stressed, and I put it down to moving because that *was* stressful, but she revealed she wasn't doing good and it wasn't all down to moving house. She was having nightmares about an incident that happened with her uncle and the brothers thirteen months ago. Keela never liked talking about what happened. I knew the gist of what went down, but not everything. I didn't know what caused Keela to be so scared… scared enough to still be having night terrors so many months after what happened.

Her nightmares weren't her only problem though. She wasn't comfortable with how fast Alec was moving with their relationship. She wanted to enjoy him in the dating game, but he wanted to get married and have babies right away.

The kicker?

Alec knew none of this. Nothing about her nightmares, and diddly-squat about her hesitation with what she wanted out of their relationship. This all came out of course… during a surprise housewarming party that Alec arranged. Keela wasn't impressed at all, she had a bit of meltdown, and if things weren't bad enough, her uncle, her cousin Micah and her husband showed up.

You know, the uncle who is really a gangster, the cousin who puts the B in bitch, and her husband who is the biggest wank stain *ever*. Yeah, those bastards. They showed up, and they caused arguments, physical fights... they even caused the *Gardai* to be called. They found out about the party thanks to my bastard little brother, Gavin. He was somehow close to Brandon and Jason now, however that situation was too fresh for me to think about right now. I needed time before I even thought about that little fucker.

The whole situation was bad, but what really put the cherry on top of our fucked-up-day-cake was the stupid thing myself, Branna, Bronagh, and Alannah did in Keela's bathroom for fun.

Before shit hit the fan, we had some drinks to unwind from a long day of packing and unpacking and we thought it would be funny to take pregnancy tests. And it *was* funny, until Keela showed up and knocked the pregnancy tests into the sink and mixed them up. That wouldn't normally be a problem, but guess what one of the test results turned out to be?

You guessed it.

One of us was fucking *pregnant*, and we had no clue who.

We had Keela to thank for that.

It got scarier when Alannah ruled herself out of possibly being pregnant because she swore there was no tick in her clock for at least six months. So that left Bronagh, Branna, or myself to have the pleasure of being with child.

Ha. Pleasure my arse.

I prayed it was either Bronagh or Branna who was pregnant, simply because those two were in committed relationships, while I wasn't. The closest I ever got to being in a relationship was the hate/hate thing I had going on with Storm—and he was a dog. And he hated me.

We were going to see who the unlucky lady was, but Keela ran out of pregnancy tests, which of course was just fucking typical. She was on her way to go get some more tests when the bastards I mentioned before showed up and things got put on the back burner for an hour or two.

Things were calm now though, and Keela went on her way to our local supermarket with Kane Slater, we don't like him, to get more tests. I was impatiently waiting for them to return and so were the lads.

All three of them—Nico, Ryder, and Alec, were sat in the sitting room of Alec and Keela's house trying to piece a fucking shattered vase back together. I knew it was a lost cause, but I came over to Ryder's house for glue when he asked for it.

I had to go the toilet though, and that's how I ended up sitting on a toilet staring at a pregnancy test. I spotted the box on the counter and it had one test left in it. I knew Branna would've obviously wanted to use it, but I had to know if it was me who was pregnant.

I had to know.

Plucking up the courage to actually check what the result was turned out to be more difficult than I anticipated.

I was about to peek at the test results when my phone buzzed for what had to be the tenth time in the last five minutes. I didn't look at it when it first rang because I thought it was Gavin, but when I took it out and glanced at the caller I saw it was Keela.

I clicked answer.

"Aideen! Finally!" Keela's voice cried.

I froze. "Keela? What's wrong? Are you okay?"

"No," she whimpered. "It's Kane, he collapsed."

My heart stopped beating, my stomach churned, my throat clogged up and my head spun. I was acutely aware of how I felt in that moment—I was absolutely terrified.

"What the hell do you mean Kane collapsed?" I shouted into the speaker of my phone after a not so long pause.

"I mean exactly that. We were in Tesco and he just dropped. No warnin', he just fell. The ambulance is here and the paramedics have him on a stretcher. I'm goin' to head to the hospital with him. Can you go to the brothers' house and tell them to get their fucking arses to the hospital right away? None of them are answerin' their bloody phones."

My voice was raspy as I asked, "What about the girls? Did you try them?"

Keela hissed. "Their phones are ringin' out too. I'm goin' to fuckin' kill them all. I'm scared shitless and *none* of them are answerin'."

I blinked my eyes and was surprised when tears fell onto my cheeks.

What the hell?

I quickly wiped under my eyes then took a few deep breaths to calm myself. I would be no good to anyone if I freaked out. I was pretty focused until my best friend showed signs that she was cracking. I squeezed my eyes shut when I heard Keela sniffle on the other end of the phone.

"It'll be okay, Kay," I said, hoping the comfort I offered helped her, because it did shit for me.

"Just get the brothers and meet me at the hospital, please."

She hung up and for a long moment I stood unmoving and tried to process what she just told me, but I couldn't, I just couldn't. It was probably best because I quickly sprung into action by jumping up and running out of the bathroom and the Slater household without a backwards glance. I sprinted across the road and crashed into Alec and Keela's front door knocking it open.

"Lads!" I screamed, as I ran into the sitting room.

"Aideen!" Ryder shouted and grabbed hold of my shoulders when I stumbled into the room. "Calm down and tell us what's wrong."

I inhaled and exhaled a couple of times trying to get my breath back, and when I did I looked from Ryder to his brothers and back again.

"Keela called me… from the supermarket."

Alec moved closer. "Is she okay?"

I nodded my head. "*She* is."

Nico moved closer too. "And Kane?"

Tears gathered in my eyes. Again

I shook my head. "She said it happened so fast. He was standin' beside her one second and on the floor the next."

All the brothers widened their eyes, and from behind them Branna and Alannah gasped.

"She tried to ring, but no one answered their phones," I continued. "She is on her way to the hospital with him, but we have to go there right now."

The next few minutes were a blur of activity with the lads shouting and the girls crying. We all ran out of Alec and Keela's new house, and piled into cars. I went with Ryder and Alec, and Nico went with the girls to get Bronagh.

"He's goin' to be okay, isn't he?" I asked the lads as Ryder flew down the bypass with Nico following close behind before he turned down the road to go get his girl.

I felt a hand grip onto my shoulder. "He *is* going to be okay."

I hadn't talked to God in a long time, not since my mother died when I was little, but on the drive to the hospital I prayed to find out what was wrong with Kane and if he was okay. I prayed harder than I ever had before, and I begged Him to let Kane be okay.

I jumped when my phone went off.

I quickly answered it, "Hello?"

"Where are you all?" Keela cried.

She was sobbing, I could hear it in her voice.

I broke down with worry. "We're nearly there… is he okay?"

The brothers held their breath when I asked the question we were all thinking.

Keela bawled, "I'm tryin' to find that out, but I'm not related to him so the brothers need to be here."

"Why?" I asked, terrified to hear her reply.

"Because they won't tell me if he is dead or alive."

ACKNOWLEDGEMENTS

I can't believe this is my fourth book in the *Slater Brothers* series that I have published. I am amazed. I am in love with this group of lads and their sassy ladies. I love writing their stories, and I can't wait for you all to dive into the rest of the brothers' books.

As usual, I had the fabulousness of my team to help me get *Keela* ready for you all to read. I would be lost without each and every one of these ladies.

My sister Edel – my outlining partner. Thank you for always supporting me and loving the brothers as much as I do. Love you.

My mini me – Thank you for allowing me time to write these books, you're the most patient five year old I know. I love you to Neptune and back!

My family – for the continued support you all give me. Thank you.

Jennifer Tovar from Gypsy Heart Editing. You're my girl, and without you publishing would never be possible. You're awesome, and make editing less grey hair inducing. Thank you for putting up with me! Love ya, babe.

Julie from JT Formatting. Thank you for making my book pretty to read, you're awesome!

Jill aka superwoman aka the world's greatest PA. Thank you for constantly being on top of your game and always looking for new ways to get the word about me, and the brothers out there. You're a dear friend, and I love you!

LJ Anderson from Mayhem Cover creations. Just like the rest of the times I've mentioned you, I have to praise and thank you. You never fail to create a cover I don't love. Thank you!

Nicola Rhead – the world's greatest proofreader. Thank you for saving my arse with Keela. You're an angel!

Yessi – my pregnant bitch. Actually by the time Keela published, the spawn of Satan you harbour in your womb will be here, but you're pregnant right now while I'm writing this so I'm not changing a thing. Deal with it. I don't like saying nice things about you, but I guess I love you. Being my best friend and all, I kind of like you. Kind of. Stop smirking! God!

Mary – my lovely, wonderful Mary. You're by far the sweetest person I know, and probably the bitchiest, which is awesome! I love your random rants of bitchiness, and I love your friendship. You're a gem, and I love you loads!

My lasses from my street team. You're all the best group of crazies I could ever wish for. Thank you for your support, and for everything you do for me. I love you all. Hard.

And most importantly my readers. Thank you for sticking by me and the brothers, I hope you liked some more from Keela and Alec. Stick around for *Kane*, he is coming soon! I love you all <3

ABOUT THE AUTHOR

L.A. Casey was born, raised and currently resides in Dublin, Ireland. She is a twenty-three year old stay at home mother to an almost two year old German Shepherd named Storm and of course, her five year old—going on thirty—beautiful little hellion/angel depending on the hour of the day.

She is the author of Amazon Bestselling book series, *Slater Brothers*.

CONNECT WITH ME

Facebook: www.facebook.com/LACaseyAuthor

Twitter: www.twitter.com/AuthorLACasey

Goodreads: www.goodreads.com/LACaseyAuthor

Website: www.lacaseyauthor.com

Email: l.a.casey@outlook.com

NOW AVAILABLE

FROZEN

DOMINIC (SLATER BROTHERS, #1)

BRONAGH (SLATER BROTHERS, #1.5)

ALEC (SLATER BROTHERS, #2)

COMING SOON

KANE (SLATER BROTHERS, #3)

AIDEEN (SLATER BROTHERS, #3.5)

RYDER (SLATER BROTHERS, #4)

BRANNA (SLATER BROTHERS, #4.5)

DAMIEN (SLATER BROTHERS, #5)

ALANNAH (SLATER BROTEHRS, #5.5)

BROTHERS (SLATER BROTHERS, #6)